COUNTDOWN TO DANGER

CHOOSE YOUR OWN ENDING!

For Danielle, Léo, Ruby, Penelope and Spooky!

Scholastic Canada Ltd.
604 King Street West, Toronto, Ontario M5V 1E1, Canada

Scholastic Inc.
557 Broadway, New York, NY 10012, USA

Scholastic Australia Pty Limited
PO Box 579, Gosford, NSW 2250, Australia

Scholastic New Zealand Limited
Private Bag 94407, Botany, Manukau 2163, New Zealand

Scholastic Children's Books
Euston House, 24 Eversholt Street, London NW1 1DB, UK

www.scholastic.ca

Library and Archives Canada Cataloguing in Publication

Szpirglas, Jeff, author
Canadian survival / Jeff Szpirglas.

(Countdown to danger)
Issued also in electronic formats.
ISBN 978-1-4431-6330-9 (softcover).--ISBN 978-1-4431-6331-6
(ebook)

1. Plot-your-own stories. 2. Choose-your-own stories.
I. Title. II. Series: Countdown to danger

PS8637.Z65C36 2018   jC813'.6   C2017-906943-8
C2017-906944-6

Photos ©: cover, title page explosion: Hubis/Shutterstock; cover, title page kayak: Denis Gorelkin/Shutterstock; cover,
title page storm: isoga/Shutterstock; cover, title page bear: Rustic/Shutterstock; cover, title page forest: Designwest/
Dreamstime; cover, title page timer: milmirko/iStockphoto; cover, 104 border: Rochakred/Dreamstime; cover water and
border throughout: Ronnie Chua/Shutterstock; digital clock used throughout: Samarskaya/iStockphoto.

6 5 4 3 2   Printed in Canada 139   19 20 21 22 23 24

JEFF SZPIRGLAS

COUNTDOWN TO
DANGER

CHOOSE YOUR OWN ENDING!

CANADIAN SURVIVAL

Scholastic Canada Ltd.
Toronto New York London Auckland Sydney
Mexico City New Delhi Hong Kong Buenos Aires

30:00

Your canoe scrapes to a halt against the rocky shore of a small lake. You wobble unsteadily out of the boat and wipe a smear of sweat from your brow. You're just steps away from a thick forest. Beyond that, a towering ring of jagged mountains surrounds you. It's like an advertisement for the Rockies.

But then reality sinks in.

You let out a shaky breath and turn around. Doubled over in the back of the canoe is Prisha Singh. She's looking pale, and a thick stream of blood oozes from a wound on her head.

She was your guide on Camp Aquila's annual canoe trip, but it's all gone wrong.

Now you're lost *and* separated from the rest of your cabin. You hadn't counted on those rapids. Why hadn't Prisha warned you?

"Prisha," you say, but she doesn't respond. You reach forward and gently pull her back. She lets out a whimper, and that's when you realize how badly hurt she is.

"Prisha," you say again, and she opens her eyes. "Why did we take those rapids? You never prepped us for them. We didn't even have the proper gear."

"We *had* to take the fork in the river," she mumbles.

"We were in danger. We were being . . . followed."

You narrow your eyes. "Followed? What are you talking about?"

"By . . ." she starts, but she's already shaking her head in disbelief. "By some kind of animal," she says.

You're about to laugh like this is some kind of weird joke, but that's when you hear something in the woods. Is it a grunting sound? It's coming from someone. Or something. It can't be very far away, either. And whatever it is, it sounds BIG. You're going to need help, and fast. When the rest of your group notices you're missing, they'll be looking for you, but who knows how long it will take them to find you out here. Prisha doesn't look like she's going to hold out too much longer without medical assistance.

You're on your own now.

Instinctively you reach into your pocket for your phone. But of course you don't get a cell signal here.

So you pull the dry bag with your emergency supplies from the canoe. Spilling the contents out, you spot a few things you'll need for sure—that map, for example. But there's also a compass, a pocket knife . . . and a flare gun!

You consider taking everything with you, but then think twice. Maybe you should leave something for Prisha. More importantly, which way should you go?

There's no time to debate this. You've got to act now.

If you grab the knife and head into the forest, turn to page 3.
If you take the flare gun and head out on the river, turn to page 4.

27:42

You grab the knife, compass and map, leaving Prisha with the flare gun, and walk towards the woods.

As soon as you step off the beach, you're swallowed in a thick coniferous forest. You're already getting scratched and covered in a film of sticky pine sap.

Plus there are the bugs.

Blackflies, mosquitoes—you name it! It's like you've walked into a cloud of insects that exist solely to drain your blood. Between dodging oncoming branches and slapping at stinging, biting insects, you're already feeling defeated.

But you're *alive.*

How long will Prisha stay that way? Or yourself, if you don't find help?

You have the feeling that there's definitely someone in these woods. But you're not going to help Prisha or yourself by waiting for them to find you. If you track them down, maybe they can help you both.

But maybe if you can get to a high vantage point, you'll have a better sense of where help might be.

If you press deeper into the woods, turn to page 5.
If you search out higher ground, turn to page 7.

27:42

"**I**'m going to take the canoe to get some help," you tell Prisha.

She nods weakly. You can tell there's no time to waste. You grab the flare gun, leaving Prisha with the knife.

Back into the canoe! You jam the paddle against the rocky shore and push off until you're floating.

You look over your shoulder and see Prisha lying on the beach. You're not sure how long she's got before something really bad happens.

Come to think of it, you're not sure how long *you've* got.

Soon you're moving downstream, and the current does most of the pushing. You just use the blade of the paddle to keep from bumping into the riverbank.

The rest of your camp group has got to be farther this way. Maybe you can catch up to them and let them know what happened.

But the river keeps flowing faster and faster. You notice that it's branching off in two directions up ahead. One way seems to be moving quickly; the other seems calmer.

The fork in the river is coming up soon. You'll need to choose which way to go—now.

If you brave the faster-moving water, turn to page 14.
If you stick to the calmer path, turn to page 15.

26:33

You head deeper into the forest and quickly realize this was a bad idea. All of your hiking experience has been on well-marked trails. There's no discernable way through this thick tangle of trees. Sharp branches jut out, poking and tearing at your skin. You try crouching down low and shimmying around the thick tree trunks, but that just makes your journey all the more confusing.

A slight crackle breaks the eerie silence. You whip your head around, looking for the source. Is it just a falling branch? Or is there someone else nearby?

You hold steady for a moment. You can feel your pulsing heartbeat in your throat and ears.

It's nothing, you try to convince yourself. You get up and move on.

And that's when you catch sight of a dark blur in the woods. It's a person, only it isn't.

It's bigger.

Darker.

And hunched over.

You blink, and then it's gone, swallowed back into the forest.

Now your heart is pounding a mile a minute. You reach into your pack for something to defend yourself with, but what? The knife? Your hand-to-hand combat skills are limited to video games, and some good that'll do you *here*.

How did a useless city slicker like you wind up here? You're about to start feeling sorry for yourself when your ears perk up at more sounds.

Something is crunching through the underbrush.

You duck behind an oversized tree trunk.

The sounds get clearer, closer.

You ignore the ticklish beads of sweat running down your brow into your eyes, and strain to get a look at whoever's coming.

Your jaw drops open.

It's Prisha!

She's looking a lot better. There's even a bandage over her head wound.

You're about to run out to her, but then you stop yourself.

How did she manage to bandage herself? She was looking close to death only a few minutes ago.

Something isn't right here. Should you stay hidden until you figure out what's going on?

If you follow Prisha from a safe distance, turn to page 9.

If you confront her right now, turn to page 12.

26:33

You turn towards the mountains and push onward and upward. Soon your muscles are working against a steep incline. Jagged rocks and boulders tear gaping holes in the mountainside. You find a few hand- and footholds and use exposed tree roots to pull yourself up, but when you look over your shoulder, you gasp. Already you're so high up that you wonder how you'll manage to get back down without falling.

Looking up again, you see that the forest soon thins out to reveal slabs of exposed rock. How are you possibly going to finish this climb?

You *must*, you tell yourself. It's do or die.

You reach forward to grab the closest root—

SNAP!

Your weight tears the root into pieces. Your footing slips. You grab on to the rock face with one hand, but you can feel your fingers slipping.

You open your mouth to scream and something GRABS YOUR WRIST.

You look up.

You're staring into the face of a man with chiselled features and a stern look on his face.

This guy is strong. With one hand, he pulls you up and sets you down beside him on the rock ledge.

He doesn't take his eyes off you for one second. He's clearly sizing you up.

Who is this guy? He's wearing camouflage clothing and has several items clipped to his vest, including some kind of futuristic-looking device that vaguely resembles a gun.

Finally, he speaks. "That was a close call," he says. "I'm John." He extends a large, weathered hand for you to shake. You tentatively reach out, and the next thing you know, he's practically crushing your hand in a vice-like grip.

If you are "Matthias," turn to page 48.

If you are "Zara," turn to page 50.

25:14

s you watch Prisha move through the forest, you're convinced that approaching her is the wrong thing to do.

For starters, she's moving fast, as if she's a) used to this wild country and b) knows where she's headed. She's also carrying a black backpack that you know wasn't in the canoe.

When you're pretty sure she's out of range, you move away from the tree. You try to follow her from a distance, but—OUCH!—you keep—ARGH!—tripping over jutting roots and scraping against scaly bark and branches. You squeeze your mouth shut and clench your fists at the pain, and then move on. You can't let Prisha get too far ahead, especially since the incline is getting steeper. You're moving up the mountainside, but to where?

You keep the best pace you can, stopping now and then to listen for Prisha. Once or twice you think you've lost her, but then you make out the faint sound of footsteps in the woods. The higher up you go, the thinner the trees and the greater the distance you need to put between you and Prisha.

Then you round a bend and stop suddenly.

The forest gives way to an immense valley. In the

distance is another mountain range with a sheer cliff face. Any sound you make will no doubt echo across the valley.

Filling the great chasm is a thick curved wall of concrete that stretches between the two mountain ranges. You've seen pictures of the Hoover Dam, and this looks just like it. On one side of the wall, a huge blue lake has formed. On the other side of the wall is a drop that's as tall as an apartment building. At the bottom, a thin river snakes through the valley.

Prisha is making her way down a rocky precipice that leads right to the top of the dam. There's no mistaking it now. This girl knows where she's going.

Prisha walks across the ridge separating the lake from the river below and stops midway. She pulls something out of the backpack. From this far away you can't see much more than some tubes and wires. Prisha digs into the pack for a rope, then lowers the object to a small ledge partway down the dam.

Once it's in place, Prisha flicks the rope, pulls it back up, and tosses it to the ground. She makes her way towards the far side of the dam, where you can see a doorway.

Wait a second. You've seen enough movies to know that this has to be some kind of bomb!

You can't stand back and do nothing.

Without thinking, you push into the open and scurry down to the top of the dam.

As you reach the ridge, your fear of heights kicks in. A fall from here would turn you into a human-sized pancake.

You shake the thought away and creep along the top of the dam. Prisha is getting closer to the doorway. But that rope she left is nearby, and you know it can at least reach the ledge where the bomb is.

If you rappel down the dam to the bomb, turn to page 16.
If you keep following Prisha, turn to page 18.

25:14

"**P**risha!" you shout.

She whips around in your direction.

Brazenly, you step out of the underbrush and stride over to her.

"What are you doing here?" she asks.

"My thoughts exactly," you snap back. "Aren't you hurt?"

She doesn't respond immediately. She looks at you and then rubs her head. That's real blood on the gauze, but she'd looked near death only moments ago.

"You left me," she starts. "I was trying to catch up with you. My head started to feel better—"

Thunk. Something falls from her pocket.

It looks like a cellphone, and you reach over to pick it up. It's actually some kind of radio with a pullout antenna.

"What's this for?"

"That's not important," Prisha says. She snatches it away from you.

You take a step back. Enough. "Who are you?" you ask.

Prisha's expression changes. She looks at you like she's trying to determine if you're a threat.

"Come on, Prisha. Now we're in this together," you tell her confidently, but you don't mean that last part. Not yet.

She lets out a long sigh. "The canoe accident was a cover to get me closer. We *were* being followed, though."

"What was following us? A beaver? A bear?"

"Something from the place we're going to. It's a top-secret facility," she says. "They're doing horrible things there, and we've got to stop it."

"We?" The more you hear, the less you like this. Plus, you're starting to wonder about that human-like shape.

"I'm with an organization that stops companies and governments from harming nature—whether it's habitats or the animals themselves. In this case, both are at risk."

She presses on, and you're forced to follow her. You're moving uphill quickly.

"For years, a private organization has been creating weaponized animals, then selling them to the highest bidder. They've been doing it right under the government's nose without being noticed. Until now. And this is a perfect window of time to stop them."

"Why?" you ask.

"The facility is going through a scheduled break. There are just a few security guards left here."

"What are you planning?" you ask.

But before Prisha can answer, the forest thins out. You step forward, and you're looking down, down, down from a high cliff. The force of your body weight starts to topple you over the edge.

Turn to page 96.
Turn to page 96.

15:29

Paddling a canoe solo isn't your strong suit, so you decide to let the faster-moving water push you to help.

The canoe thumps against a rock and water splashes you. You push off the rock and speed on. So far, so good.

Soon the shimmering waters are broken by sharp, clunky rocks. The river bubbles and froths around boulders, and the canoe speeds downstream. You're heading into rapids once again.

BAM! You slam into one boulder, and then another.

You grit your teeth. The canoe isn't designed for this kind of beating, and your life jacket won't save you from the jagged rocks if you're thrown overboard.

Suddenly you drop down a small waterfall. Your stomach sinks. The canoe tips dangerously in the rapids. There's no way to bank it safely now; you'd be dashed to pieces on the rocks.

Then you notice trees up ahead. There's one branch hanging across the river. It might just be possible to grab it and pull yourself to safety. But that means ditching the canoe . . .

If you make a grab for the branch, turn to page 20.

If you stay in the canoe and brave the rapids, turn to page 127.

15:29

Slow and steady it is. You push your paddle against the water, forcing the canoe ahead in small spurts.

You do this again and again, and it's not long before you have to pull the paddle back over the canoe and pant for breath.

You were exhausted before this second leg of the journey, and there's no telling how long you'll have to keep this up.

You're about to sink the paddle back into the water when you hear a sound in the distance. The more you strain to hear it, the more you can discern rushing water.

You look ahead. There don't appear to be any rapids.

No. Not rapids. But the current is moving more quickly now. You're making good progress without even paddling.

"Sweet," you say to yourself. You lie back in the canoe and put your hands behind your head.

You close your eyes—just for a second—listening to the sound of rushing water—

"GRRRRRNG!"

Startled, you nearly jump out of the canoe. Instead you bang your head against the side and peer over the edge.

No—it can't be!

Turn to page 41.

18:55

You lean over the edge of the dam and the world starts to spin. You imagine plummeting to the river below, and you wonder what would kill you first: the impact or the shock of falling.

Then you spot the dark object sitting on a ledge twenty or thirty metres below. There's no mistaking the small digital panel and the red and blue wires. *It's like a movie bomb*, you think to yourself, and almost laugh at how ridiculous this all seems.

If that bomb goes off, what happens to the dam? What about the other kids on your canoe trip? Blowing up the dam puts them all in danger.

You look over your shoulder to the coil of rope. There's no time to think about why Prisha left it there. You need to take advantage of it now.

Hands sweating, you pull the rope over to the edge of the dam. You've never taken a knot-tying course, and you spent way too long with Velcro shoes. Now you've got to knot yourself a lifeline.

You find a pipe jutting out of the side of the dam and wind the cord around it. Your first knot comes apart when you tug on it. Not good.

"The bunny goes through the hole," you tell yourself.

A few more tries and you give the rope a good yank. It holds, and you pump your fist in the air. "Yes!" you yelp. But will the rope hold your entire body weight?

No time to think about failure, either.

You toss the remainder of the rope over the edge, then reconsider. What if you let go? Better to wrap it around one of your wrists and inch your way down. At least then you'll be secured to *something*.

With that in mind, you clutch the rope and turn around so you're facing away from the perilous drop. Your wrists are so soaked with sweat you fear the rope might slip—but this is what must be done. You lower yourself over the precipice.

Your feet press against the vertical wall. Without looking down, you push off the wall and let a tiny coil of rope loose.

You unfurl a bit more rope from around your wrist, and inch down. You worry that you might not have much time before the bomb goes off, and wonder if you should pick up the pace.

If you keep inching down, turn to page 26.
If you start to rappel more quickly, turn to page 27.

18:55

If Prisha's going to leave that bomb by the dam and head inside, your best bet is to stick close by.

You crouch low to the ground and follow her towards the door.

Prisha pulls something out of her pocket. It's small and fits into the palm of her hand. She runs it across the door, and you hear an audible *ping* as the door slides open.

Prisha enters, and for a second, the door remains temptingly open.

It's now or never.

You get up and sprint forward.

You're just a metre away when the door begins to slide closed. You push yourself forward at full tilt. A second later the door shuts behind you with a heavy clank. You shake your arms, just to check that they haven't been sliced off by the metal door.

Darkness surrounds you. You can't see or hear Prisha anywhere, which is good, you think. You're safely inside whatever this place is. The only problem is that you're also trapped in it!

Turn to page 25.

01:33

You edge closer and closer to John, trying to get in throwing range. Then, when you're ready, you pull the pocket knife out of your pocket, flick the blade open, and hurl it towards John. "Take that!" you shout.

You watch the knife sail through the air.

And miss John completely.

It lands with a tiny thud.

John turns to you. "Really?" he says. "You were going to stop me by throwing *that*?"

You look at the tiny knife. Then you watch as the wolverines get even closer. You turn back to John. "Uhhh . . . Can I have a do-over?"

"Sadly, no," John says. Then he presses a button on the remote and steps aside. The wolverines leap in unison.

It's a pretty amazing sight. The wolverines twist and turn in the air, their massive claws outstretched, all coming right at you. This is exactly the sort of thing that would blow your mind in a nature documentary. But now it's happening in real life, right in front of your eyes.

Too bad you won't live to tell this story.

THE END.

To try again, go back to page 48.

08:28

As the canoe speeds closer to the overhanging branch, you turn your attention away from the bone-crunching rocks and raging waters, and zero in on your lifeline.

Slowly, you move into a crouch, extending your wobbly arms for balance. There's just one shot at this. Miss, and you'll either drown or be torn to gory pieces.

It's a fifty-fifty shot (though come to think of it, maybe more like ninety-ten, in favour of near-certain death). You wait until the branch is directly overhead, and then you leap.

Turn to page 23 . . .
. . . or page 45.

01:33

ithout warning, you flip the knife open and fling it at John.

It snaps through the air and slices his hand. He screams, drops the remote, and grabs his hand.

"Awesome!" you yell. The remote is lying on the ground, and you dive towards it, arms outstretched. You snatch it up and back away from John.

Around you, the circle of wolverines waits patiently.

"Nice throw," John admits. "Now give me that remote so I can keep us both safe from these animals."

"Uh-huh," you say. "I don't think so. You'll just turn them back on me."

You back up farther and one of the wolverines snaps at you. You dodge its sharp teeth and edge around the circle.

John creeps towards you. He does a trick with the knife so that it flips around his hand, then he catches the handle and jabs the blade at you. He's trying to scare you and it works. Still, you've got the upper hand. You glance down at the remote.

"You're holding an expensive piece of equipment. It's been carefully calibrated, Matthias. Please hand it over. There are only a handful of people in the world who can operate it successfully."

You look back down at the remote. "I can work this," you say.

"Matthias, you play with that and we're both dead."

Maybe, but you don't have much to lose at this point. You press a button and move the joystick. The wolverines turn their attention to the trees. You flip the joystick again, and they angle their jaws at you. Another flip, and they're facing John. John gulps.

This advanced technology seems intuitive. You start to toy with the remote, getting the wolverines to jump and roll over. "Sweet!" you shout. "My own army of wolverines!"

John turns to run, and you quickly surround him with wolverines.

"I may not have years of army training, but I bet I've spent more time playing video games than you."

John tries to back away from the wolverines, but you close the circle on him.

"Game on," you tell him.

Now you've got your own personal army of wolverines, and you've just stopped some crazy mercenary. Maybe it's turning out to be a good day after all.

Plus, wait'll Prisha gets a load of your new pets . . .

00:00

You survived! There are ten other ways to escape the danger—try to find them all!

07:56

Y ou jump.

It's the kind of no-brain plan that will get you killed. You're no basketball prodigy. You're just a kid in an out-of-control canoe—

CRIPES, IT WORKED!

You're dangling in the air, hanging on to the branch for dear life. You watch as the canoe is pushed down the rapids and smashed to pieces. That could have been you.

You look down at the violently foaming river. You clutch the branch and shimmy your way across until you're over dry land.

It's anything but graceful, but as you land in a painful heap on the muddy riverbank, you realize: *I'm alive!*

Next thought: *Why didn't I have someone around to record that amazing jump? I could have had, like, three million YouTube hits!*

Another thought: *Wow, I'm totally hungry. My stomach is really growling.*

New thought: *Not hungry. Not my stomach.*

Then: *Something is definitely growling, and it's not coming from me.*

At this point you pick out a shaggy shape in your periphery. You pivot, trying to keep as still as possible.

You're several metres away from a massive grizzly. The thing is built like a brick house. The bear bellows at you. You've definitely invaded its turf.

The bear lurches forward. Your gaze shifts from its beady eyes to the sharp claws jutting out from its paws.

You think about all the things you've heard about bear attacks. Make yourself look bigger than this bear? It's easily three times your height. Crouch into a ball? That sounds ridiculous.

Run away as fast as you can? *Yes*, you decide. If you can jump from a canoe to a branch, then maybe you can outrun a bear.

You whirl around, take a few steps, and—

There's a sasquatch standing in front of you.

Yup. Sasquatch.

Big. Hairy. Standing on two legs.

And definitely not a grizzly bear.

Your mind races. Aren't sasquatches imaginary? How did one get here? More importantly: How did you get between it and a bear? Finally: How are you going to get out of this one? There's nowhere else to run. You've got the raging river behind you. The bear and the sasquatch are blocking any other escape route. You tense your body, ready to spring into action. You're going to have to go around one of them.

If you try to outrun the bear, turn to page 133.

If you try to dodge the sasquatch, turn to page 32.

18:26

radually, your eyes adjust to the darkness. You're standing on a metal grille. There are floors above and below you. You take a cautious step forward, trying to make as little noise as possible, and follow the one source of light. It illuminates a staircase that winds both up and down at the back of the room.

You wonder why the lights are so low. Maybe the base is closed today? If Prisha is trying to get inside without being detected, then that could make sense.

But where is she? And why is she here?

You stop and hold your breath. Footsteps echo from somewhere below you.

You'll have to tread lightly.

After descending a few floors, you reach a level that's more brightly lit. Instead of just a dark catwalk, you find a corridor illuminated by fluorescent bulbs. A mechanical hum is coming from somewhere.

But your ears perk up at the sound of footsteps on the staircase. Prisha hasn't stopped here. Maybe you shouldn't either.

If you try to find Prisha, turn to page 37.
If you investigate what's on this floor instead, turn to page 39.

13:30

There's no point in getting reckless, especially when you're this close to the bomb. Besides, it's not likely to go off with Prisha still nearby.

You've still got the rope coiled tightly around your wrist. If you can unwind it a bit at a time—just like you're doing right now—then you'll make it to the ledge. At the very least, you can throw the bomb down to the river, away from the dam, and—

You feel the rope grow slack.

There's a sinking feeling in your stomach. You look up.

The knot. It wasn't tied as securely as you thought.

And then you're falling.

The ledge speeds past you. You reach out for it, but your view starts shifting from the massive wall of the dam to the little river down below. Maybe not so little anymore.

And all that goes through your mind as you hurtle downward is the gnawing thought that you should have taken more time to learn how to tie your shoes, and tie a good knot.

THE END.

To try again, go back to page 9.

13:30

You're not sure what you trust less—that bomb below or whether you've tied a strong enough knot.

In any case, speed trumps caution. You twirl your wrist so the rope unwinds in quick thrusts. You're moving fast. Heart in your throat, you fear the worst—that you're either going to fall to your death or explode with the bomb.

Then your feet touch solid ground. Holy moly—you've hit the ledge!

You feel a surge of adrenalin course through your body, and you shakily bend down to inspect the bomb.

You see wires—red and blue—coming out of the bomb but you can't take your eyes off the timer. It's at the twelve-minute mark, and counting down. What could Prisha be doing on the other side of that door?

Who cares? Bigger question: How do you disarm a bomb?

You fumble in your pocket. All you have is that pocket knife you pulled out of the canoe. But is it sharp enough to slice through wire? And which wire should you cut?

Already a minute's gone by, and the timer is still counting down—

If you cut the red wire, turn to page 30.
If you cut the blue wire, turn to page 31.

02:21

You give Prisha a head start and pull yourself back onto the Jet Ski.

Inertia throws you back as you put it to full throttle, but you grip the handles tightly and roar away. You've never ridden one of these things before today, but you're starting to get the hang of it.

There! As you round a bend you see Prisha up ahead.

You push the Jet Ski to its limit. You're moving so quickly that you skip across the surface of the water like Thor himself has flung you.

As long as you hold the Jet Ski steady, you'll catch up.

Your arms tense. You don't even wipe away the water that keeps splashing you in the face. You just narrow your eyes to slits and squint at the fast-approaching object.

Full speed, you think.

Or did they call it "ramming speed"?

Prisha turns and spots you, but it's too late.

You're close enough that you can see her eyes widen. Her mouth drops. She looks like she's trying to warn you about something, but you've already ditched the Jet Ski and are flying through the air.

You look down from high above as your Jet Ski SMASHES into the back of hers.

A huge fireball ripples into the air, but you're still out of range. You cover your head and splash down, narrowly avoiding the flaming Jet Ski fragments.

And then you start to swim to shore.

Prisha's doing the same. She heaves herself onto the rocky shoreline, coughing up water and looking worse for the wear. She watches you swim up, but you're both unarmed. What's she going to do now?

"You fool!" she shouts. "Now we're stuck here!"

"Yup," you breathe, taking in a gulp of air and feeling satisfied at being far away from the dam.

"Then why are you so happy?"

"Because," you say, "we're going to get rescued. Someone's going to notice that the dam burst. I bet you a rescue team's probably on its way right now."

You're only half-sure of this, but judging from the look on Prisha's face, she thinks you're right.

Prisha gets up and takes a few steps, probably thinking about disappearing into the thick forest, but she's limping and exhausted.

"Yeah, I wouldn't get too far on my own, either," you tell her. Then you think about the last half hour and give a shrug. "Or would I?"

00:00

You survived! There are ten other ways to escape the danger— try to find them all!

11:04

You crouch down so you're facing the bomb. But as you lean closer to the red wire, the knife begins to shake in your sweaty hands.

You've got a fifty-fifty shot at this, and now you're thinking those odds aren't great.

The heck with it. You put some pressure on the bomb with one hand, and reach the blade of the knife under the red wire with the other. Taking a deep breath, you pull back on the knife and—

CLICK. The blade pulls through the wire, and—

The timer on the clock starts counting down even more quickly.

"What?"

Ten minutes? Bah! More like one at the rate the clock is speeding down.

Who designs a timer that goes faster when you cut the wires? Why are those wires even there in the first place? To give people false hope?

You stand up and toss the knife aside. There's no way you can run away from this thing.

And then a loud sound jolts you:

BLANG! BLANG! BLANG!

Turn to page 90.

You've seen a gazillion movies where people cut the red wire, and they ALWAYS EXPLODE!

No way that's going to be you. Blue wire it is!

Focus, you tell yourself. Blue wire. Knife. Cut.

You carefully tease the blue wire apart from the red one, but the wire, you realize, is getting tangled. You give it a little tug, but you end up pulling the red wire too.

Maybe just a little more of a tug. Just . . .

Pop! Both wires get yanked out of the side of the bomb.

Your stomach starts to spin.

You squeeze your eyes shut, take a deep breath, and—

Nothing.

You open them again. Still here. Even with that red wire out, neither the bomb nor you has exploded.

And then you see the timer.

The countdown is moving at high speed now. There were ten minutes left, but now it's more like one.

Cripes, who designed this thing?

You stand up, reeling around. What are you going to do now?

And then you're startled by a massive sound:

BLANG! BLANG! BLANG!

Turn to page 90.

03:19

Y ou don't stand much of a chance against either creature, but at least the sasquatch doesn't appear to have
claws. It's definitely stronger than you, but is it faster?

Only one way to find out.

And what better way to use the element of surprise?
You shake your butt and yell out "sasquatch THIS!" then
dodge out of the way.

The sasquatch lunges at you.

You scream. Bad idea! You try to twist out of its
path, but the sasquatch moves with astounding
speed. You brace yourself as it reaches back with a
shaggy hand.

BOOF!

You collapse.

It wasn't as painful as you expected. You turn around
and see why.

The bear is taking a swipe at the sasquatch, which
ducks out of the way. The sasquatch shoots you a glance,
furrows its thick brow, and grumbles something unin-
telligible. "GRRRGLGRRRG!" it roars.

You're still sitting there, astounded. "Wha—?"

"GRRRRRG!" it grrrrrgs again, which you interpret
as: *Just sit down and shut it.*

Then the bear rears back up. The sasquatch sidesteps it, tensing its thick fists.

Oh man, you realize. Not only did that sasquatch just save your skin from the bear, but you're now sitting ringside at the craziest boxing/mixed martial arts match in the entire history of nature. Where is your camera when you need it?

It really is like something out of *King Kong vs. Godzilla.* You scramble out of the way as the two giants duke it out. They exchange blows so quickly and violently that you're soon losing sight of which one's winning. It's a whirl of fur, hair, teeth, claws and blood.

It's also the distraction that you need.

Keeping your eyes locked on the melee, you begin to creep back into the forest. Maybe you'll be able to slip away unnoticed.

THWIP!

An echo rings through the forest.

THWIP! THWIP!

From behind, you hear a high-pitched whine. The bear scampers away on all fours.

The sasquatch stands there, body tensed, scanning the dense foliage for any sign of movement.

You freeze in place.

THWIP!

The sasquatch lets out a painful yelp. You both notice the yellow-tipped dart sticking out of its arm.

The sasquatch yanks it out like a toothpick, then searches through the forest and gives the kind of roar that shakes the needles from the pines.

THWIP! THWIP!

Two more darts embed in the sasquatch's thick fur. It tears them out and roars some more, but its steps are ragged. It stumbles about, eyes slowly glazing over.

Then you hear cracks and snaps in the forest. Armed guards approach, seemingly from all sides.

How are you going to escape this one? You should have run while you had the chance, instead of sitting down for what was admittedly a way-cool spectator sport.

The sasquatch pitches forward. There's a heavy *WHUMP* as it hits the earth, letting out an exhausted groan.

THWIP!

Pain suddenly flares along your leg. You look down and spot the yellow dart jutting out of your thigh. Your heart begins to race. You make a grab for the dart, but your fingers are growing cold and numb.

You look at the figures moving your way, but they're getting blurry, darker . . .

"Looks like we've got ourselves another one," you hear a man call out.

Go to the next page.

L ight.
Bright. Searing.

You try to close your eyes, but wait—they're *already* closed. You try to blink the light away, but your eyes just fill with tears. You try to wipe the tears away . . . but your hands don't move.

You try again. There's resistance against your wrists. Come to think of it, there's resistance against your legs too. You pull and pull, but the restraints bite against your skin. Panic rushes up your stomach in a nauseous wave.

"Help!" you blurt. "Help me! I'm stuck! Somebody help me!"

Images flash in your mind: Guards. Tranquilizer darts.

How long have you been here? Come to think of it, where *is* here?

You're strapped to a metal table. The rest of the room is dark, but you start to discern shapes around you. A tray of surgical equipment lies to your side. It looks clean and shiny, suggesting nobody's used it. *Yet*.

Beyond it, you make out several other surgical tables. To the other side, a familiar image greets you. It's your body, shrouded in white. You realize you're staring into a huge mirror.

In the reflection, you spot movement off to the side.

Another "patient" is on one of the surgical tables, only this one's considerably hairier, bigger—

"Sasquatch," you whisper. The sasquatch is coming to, even though it was likely pumped with a thousand times more tranquilizer than you.

There's nothing you can do as the sasquatch begins to roar and bark madly. It tries to tear at its restraints, but it's no use. Like you, the sasquatch is a prisoner. But why? And whose?

You've got to get out of here. Fast.

That's when you notice how close your fingers are to one of the scalpels on the tray beside you. You try to inch your hand over. Just a little bit farther . . .

The sasquatch is still having a massive temper tantrum.

"Shhh!" you blurt to the animal.

It stops, finally seeming to notice you.

There! You've got the scalpel!

But what to do with it? You can't manipulate it in your hand to cut through the wrist strap. But you could wedge it between some of the other equipment on the table . . .

You've done it! The blade is close enough to the strap to cut it if you wiggle your wrist back and forth.

Turn to page 84.

10:41

Prisha's moving somewhere with purpose. Where?
You descend the staircase, treading as carefully as you can, but you're not trained in espionage. Your shoes clunk against the stairs with the grace of a herd of elephants wearing clogs.

Then, out of the corner of your eye, you spot a blur of movement.

There's Prisha, moving stealthily down a corridor that looks like every other corridor in this place. You duck behind the stairwell so Prisha won't see you if she happens to look back.

From the relative security of the stairs, you watch her enter a number into a keypad, which unlocks a metal door at the far end of the hallway. She disappears into a room.

The door begins to close.

Urgh! You're going to have to make a break for it! What is it with the doors in this place? It's got to be the least accessible evil compound in the history of evil compounds.

You race down the hallway at full speed. Time seems to move in slow motion. You watch the door continue to swing closed. You're moving steadily towards it, but if you keep up at this rate, it'll shut before you can get past it.

Unless . . .

You've played several years of Little League baseball. This is just like sliding into first—only instead of a base, you're aiming for a heavy metal door that may snap shut on part of your body, like an arm, or perhaps your neck.

But it's the only way you're going to find out what's on the other side, and what Prisha's up to.

Then again, *you're* the boss of you. You don't have to slide into anything. You could just stop running, turn around, and try to get out of this place.

If you try sliding into the room, turn to page 129.

If you turn around and get out of here while you can, turn to page 46.

10:41

Congratulations! You chose the corridor! And *what* a corridor you've chosen. It turns out to be an amazing, exciting, mind-blowing . . .

. . . corridor.

So, not at all amazing, exciting or remotely mind-blowing, unless your mind is the kind that gets blown by long stretches of hallway.

Nevertheless you're completely on edge, because this place is designed like a war bunker. You pass sets of heavy metal doors lining the hallway. They're all secured with thick rivets. And each door has a pair of lights, one green and one red, above it. All of the red lights are glowing. You decide to try a door, and give the handle a good yank. Locked.

What *is* this place? All of the locked doors suggest it's more than just a dam. You've been moving along the corridor for some time now, and this place can't just be inside the dam itself. You must be in some sort of weird compound that's built into the side of the mountain.

Wherever you are, it's not the kind of place that looks like it welcomes strangers. You'll have to keep your guard up, and you definitely don't want to get lost.

And even though you haven't spotted anyone in the

corridor, you're pretty sure someone should have spotted you by now—a series of cameras are mounted along the ceiling.

But no alarm has sounded. Perhaps Prisha has somehow disarmed the cameras and alarms, since she's sneaking around this place too.

That's when you come to a fork in the corridor. Looking down the left path, you notice a green tinge coming from the hallway. Could that mean one of the doors is unlocked?

If you take the left fork, turn to page 69.

If you continue on to the right, turn to page 73.

04:11

Keeping pace with you on the side of the river is a towering dark shape. It's walking on two shaggy legs and pointing at you with a massive hand. You've seen this kind of creature in pictures before, but never in real life. Because in real life they don't exist.

"Bigfoot!" you hear yourself exclaim.

Or is it a yeti?

Doesn't matter. Whatever that thing is, you're only a few metres away from it. It's big and powerful and making a real scene.

Now the sasquatch is pointing downstream, then back to you, then to the riverbank where it's standing. And come to think of it, that rushing-water sound is getting louder and louder by the second.

Is it trying to warn you about something? Maybe even help you? Or is it just luring you in for the kill?

You could try and figure out what, if anything, the sasquatch is trying to tell you. Or you could just stay in the water and hope it leaves you alone.

If you listen to the sasquatch, turn to page 118.
If you stay in your canoe, turn to page 121.

02:50

Forget that door. You're going to try the corridor, even if it is dark. And ominous. And exactly the kind of corridor you're likely never to return from.

You take a few tentative steps. There's very little light here. In fact, there's none at all. Any light is coming from the open door behind you.

It's hard to see, but you can hear. There's a hum coming from the end of the corridor. And as you continue working your way into the darkness, your eyes adjust to the dim light.

There it is! At the back of the corridor—the switch!

There's no mistaking the massive breaker. Only you can't exactly flick this thing. It's easily the size of your arm.

So you shove all of your weight down on it.

It barely moves.

What are you going to do? There's nothing big and heavy to knock it down with—except yourself.

You walk back to the door, stretch out your arms, and take a running start towards the switch. You can't see it, so you blindly leap, flinging yourself towards the far wall, and—

The switch slams down, taking you to the floor with it.

"Yes!" you bellow.

And then ALL OF THE LIGHTS GO OFF.

"Oh," you say.

It worked. But now you're trapped in pitch blackness, with nothing to guide you back.

Alarms start to blare. Are they close by?

You get up, take a few steps, and bump into something cold and hard.

"Wall," you say.

Right. *Don't do that again,* you tell yourself.

WHUMP!

"Wall."

WHUMP!

"Wall."

How far are you? You can't tell. But as you keep saying "wall" with every bump, you hear your voice echo more and more, as if you're headed back to the exhaust chamber—

You pitch forward.

Fan blades!

Your arms shoot out. You're falling, going to hit the fan blades—

You catch the cord.

You grip it tightly as the rest of your body topples over. Your legs sail in the air, but you hold on for dear life.

You scream. The sound must carry upward, because a moment later you feel yourself moving in that direction.

Centimetre by centimetre you go, until the light

above you changes from a small white orb to an all-enveloping glow. You start to make out the trees around you, and then you're over the edge.

You grab hold of the metal grate and pull yourself back onto solid ground.

John sits there, heaving for breath and glistening with sweat.

"Nice one, kid," he says.

"Prisha," you say, uncertainly.

He shakes his head and smiles. "I don't know who you are, but you've got guts. Come on," he says, getting to his feet. "We've got to make tracks. Our agents are already in position."

Our?

You look over your shoulder. You see the dam in the distance. Small figures are rappelling down the mountainside. An army of mercenaries have emerged from the woods, and they're making their assault on the base. All thanks to you.

Yes, you.

You're not sure if that's a good thing, but as John leads you deeper into the woods, you realize you're about to find out.

00:00

You survived! There are ten other ways to escape the danger—try to find them all!

07:56

You erupt out of the canoe and into the air.

Time slows to a near standstill. You watch the canoe shrink away as you rise in the air like an NBA star about to slam-dunk. You look up, see the branch coming your way, and reach out to grasp it.

It's coming closer.

And closer.

You sail through the air. You make a desperate grab. But you're grasping at *nothing*!

And then, as surely as you took to the air, you're coming down. Fast.

The canoe is already downstream. You watch as it hits the rocks ahead.

SMASH! The hull cracks in half with a deafening thud. Then the two pieces splinter into fragments.

You hurtle back down, splashing into the water.

It's alarmingly cold. All you can let out is a watery gurgle as your open mouth is drenched in white spray.

There is no help for you, not *ever*, as you barrel towards the rocks . . .

THE END.

To try again, go back to page 4.

06:24

ope. You can't make that slide without getting crushed to a bloody pulp.

You skid to a stop, then turn around. You notice there's a red light above each door lining the hall. Except one door, which has a green light.

The green light sounds like a plan. You try the door, and the handle turns. "Sweet!" you say to yourself.

You take a step in and realize what a mistake this was.

The room is full of medical equipment and people wearing white lab coats. On a table in front of you is some kind of large, hairy . . . animal?

The door shuts behind you with a heavy clunk. All eyes in the room flick over to you. Whoops!

There's a moment of silence, and you realize you should say something. Like, anything. So you blurt out the first thing that pops into your mind. "Did anyone order a pizza?" you try. More silence.

"Who are you?"

"Too late! He's seen the experiment."

Experiment? What are they talking about?

"Release the beaver!" someone yells. Then the scientists all break away from the table and run through an open door at the other end of the room.

You, meanwhile, turn around and try the door you entered through, but it won't budge. You're locked in!

You turn back around only to discover that all of the scientists have sealed themselves into a glass booth at the back of the room, leaving you alone with . . .

. . . that large, hairy thing on the table. And it's moving.

It slides off the table and lands on all fours.

Is it some kind of bear? How are you going to defend yourself against a bear—

SLAP! A massive tail thwacks the concrete floor.

You scream. It's not a bear.

It's impossible! Before you stands a bear-sized beaver. That cute little animal on the five-cent coin isn't looking so cute anymore.

Why is it so big? More importantly, why does it have a giant pair of fangs for teeth?

You back away, but you have nowhere to go. The over-sized vampire rodent comes lumbering towards you, thick drool dripping from its fangs.

Then the creature leaps up on two legs and pins you under its massive bulk. Fur presses into your face—up your nostrils, into your open, screaming mouth.

And then you feel those huge fangs scrape along your neck.

THE END.
To try again, go back to page 25.

12:08

"I'm Matthias," you say, wincing at the force John's using. Is that intentional? Is he trying to tell you how tough he is, because you're pretty sure you got that part already.

"Strange place for a hike," John says. He hands you a canteen, and you practically douse your face with water trying to get it down.

"Easy, easy," he says. "Try to get some down your throat. It's more useful there."

"I'm sorry," you pant between gulps. It takes you about ten seconds to finish what's left, and then you're heaving for breath on the mountainside with a stranger. An armed stranger.

John—if that's his real name—scans the woods around you. "You up here alone?"

You definitely don't trust this guy, and your gut tells you not to say too much just yet. "I'm with a group," you say, which isn't a lie. "The others aren't too far behind."

"It's a pretty remote place to be climbing without proper gear," he says. Then he fixes you with a long glance. "I hope your group is better prepared."

"Oh, they are," you say way too quickly. "I should probably get back to them."

"Why don't I help you find them," he returns. "You don't look like you know this country. Otherwise you'd be properly equipped for it. Don't worry. I know my way around here."

The more John talks, the less you like it. What's he doing out here all by himself anyhow? And why? You need to get help for Prisha, but trusting John might get you into even deeper trouble. You keep glancing at that device on his hip and trying not to stare, but your heart is thumping like mad.

Maybe you should just trust him. You don't know how much longer Prisha will last. But maybe you're better off getting away from "John" as fast as you can.

If you run away, turn to page 53.

If you go along with John, turn to page 54.

12:08

You're about to introduce yourself, but John beats you to it. "I know we haven't met before, but I understand you were working undercover in that summer camp," he says. And then: "Were you followed?"

You look at him blankly. Followed? What?

Suddenly it hits you: *HE THINKS YOU'RE PRISHA.*

Then, another realization: *PRISHA ISN'T A CANOE TRIPPER. SHE'S WORKING WITH THIS GUY.*

And most importantly: *THIS GUY IS ARMED.*

You try to suppress the heavy waves of panic rolling through your system. You swallow and shake your head. "It's just me," you say.

"Well, Ms. Singh," he says, "I thought you'd look a little older given your experience, but that's quite the climb you've made in record time."

You look back down the mountain and have to agree with him. "Just doing my job," you venture.

He reaches out a hand to pull you to your feet. "The organization tells me that you're an expert at aerial feats. As you know, I'll be your point man. Let me take you to our site, and we can go from there."

"Sure thing," you say, and follow him along the rocky ledge.

What is this guy going on about? Organization? Aerial feats? What have you stumbled into?

As gripped with fear as you are, part of you wants to know more. You do your best to follow John along the mountainside, but that means not freaking out every time you catch a dizzying view of the cliffs that drop straight down to the abyss below.

It's a good thing your stomach is almost empty—otherwise you'd be heaving up your lunch right now.

John rounds a corner. You follow him, then stop in your tracks.

You're looking down at a dam. The giant wall of concrete stretches from one side of the mountain all the way across the valley to another mountain. "I know. It's impressive that a rogue consortium was able to build this complex and keep it secret for so many years," John says. "Of course, that all ends today."

"Yeah," you say, trying to keep up the conversation. "We're going to stop it."

"I mean, can you believe anyone would be experimenting with animals like this? Creating freakish hybrids and weaponizing them? The experiments going on in that place are almost unthinkable—pushing the very fringes of known science."

Animal hybrids as weapons?

"I know. It's awful," you say.

John kneels down by a set of backpacks. He unzips

one and pulls out a bunch of gear that looks like high-tech gadgetry from a spy movie. What's he up to? More to the point, what's *Prisha* supposed to be up to?

"I love animals," you try. "They're the best." Wow. You sound like a real birdbrain.

John breaks away from his work and whirls around to face you. He has an angry look on his face. Oh, great. You've just given yourself away with that stupid line. He looks like he's about to reach for his weapon—

"The world needs more people like you, Prisha. I'm so proud to be working alongside you."

Your mouth had been open to scream, but instead you give a tiny little "Oh." And then, "Thanks."

He's already turned away from you. He grabs something from the ground, and turns to show it to you. It's one of the backpacks.

"Cool," you tell him.

"Let's get you ready for the big jump," he says.

Jump?

Then you notice the cords coming out the sides of the backpack.

Turn to page 78.

09:47

You turn to John and utter the first excuse that comes to mind: "I need a bathroom break. Be back in a jiffy!"

You walk away as casually as possible. That was as good an excuse as any, wasn't it?

ZAP! ZAP! Laser beams blast into the tree in front of you, and burnt bark chips flutter downward to your head.

"Lasers!" you blurt, amazed and horrified.

"Quieter than bullets," John muses coolly. "And good for cleaning up unwanted messes," he says, aiming the blaster at you.

You drop and roll, avoiding the next wave of lasers. You can't blame John for not buying your crummy excuse.

ZAP! This beam is way too close for comfort. You bolt into the woods and zigzag around the dense foliage. Up ahead are large, exposed rocks. They would provide you with some cover, but you'd have to make it there first.

You've got the head start, but John knows how to manoeuvre around the woods, and he's armed. You won't last long at this rate.

Unless . . . Unless you do something totally crazy, like fling yourself down the mountainside.

If you make the leap, turn to page 122.

If you make a break for the boulders, turn to page 125.

09:47

"Whatever you say, John."

Best to play this as cool as you can. You follow John back into the forest. Maybe he can help you get back to Prisha, and help her out. He seems like the kind of guy who knows how to survive in these woods.

Yup, this guy definitely knows the woods. You keep getting scratched and scraped by twigs and branches, but he moves like some kind of forest ninja, ducking and twisting his way through the sharp tangle of branches without getting a single scratch. Maybe this wasn't such a good idea after all.

Once you're deeper in the woods, John stops and turns to you. "You're trying to decide how safe I am right now, aren't you?"

"Huh?"

"Well, now that we're away from any possibility of a group that you may or may not be inventing, I think we can be frank with one another. Can't we, Matthias?"

"Uh . . ." you say.

"Mmm-hmm," John nods. "So, let's get a few things sorted out. Yes, I've had army training, and no, I don't work for them anymore. Yes, I'm using that training to take care of some business up here, and no, you were not part of the plan."

"What kind of business?" you ask.

John doesn't answer. Instead, he unclips something from his belt. It's a metal box of some sort, with a few buttons and knobs. John holds it in one hand and extends an antenna with the other.

The uneasy silence continues.

"What's that?" you ask.

But John doesn't even look at you. He's too busy fiddling with the controls of whatever this thing is.

"Is that for some kind of drone?" you ask. That makes sense, doesn't it? Maybe he's using it for superspy stuff and he can get a really good view from up here on the mountain. Yes, that's *got* to be it.

"Nice try, but wrong," John says.

You hear twigs snap and crackle. Something's moving through the underbrush. Instinctively, you back up towards John. He doesn't look nervous. In fact, he looks like this is *exactly* what he expected.

Then a dark, hairy shape pushes into a clearing in the forest.

At first you think it's a large dog. But its fur and markings are all wrong. The ears are too short, and the tail too long and bushy. Not to mention its huge sharp claws.

"She's beautiful, isn't she?" John says.

"What is it?"

"Wolverines," John tells you, a glint in his eye.

"But there's only one," you say.

John shakes his head.

A second or two later, you hear more rustling in the woods. Five more wolverines slink into the clearing. They're all facing you, and now they're growling to reveal razor-sharp teeth.

John steps away from you.

"Like I said, Matthias, I'm sorry, but you're really not part of the plan."

He presses a button on the remote. The wolverines move into position.

You glance from the oncoming wolverines to John, and the remote in his hand.

Is he controlling them? No way! That's impossible!

Still, you're close enough that you might be able to make a grab for the remote. Then again, maybe you should just run.

If you try to get the remote away from John, turn to page 114.

If you run, turn to page 106.

01:35

Like you're NOT going to press a giant red button labelled *EMERGENCY*. That's what this is, isn't it?

You let the guard put a few more paces between you. Then you bolt over to the control panel and slam your fist down on the button.

Instantly the room is bathed with red light.

A loud alarm starts blaring. You jump. The guard jumps. The cell doors hiss, and then swing open simultaneously.

It takes a few seconds for the guard to realize what's happening, but that's all the time you need.

"You fool!" the guard shouts, but you're already running at breakneck speed. He's all the way at the other end of the lab/operating room/whatever the heck this place is.

Out of the corner of your eye you see animals fleeing their enclosures. That bear-moose hybrid. The giant sabre-toothed beaver-crab. Others too: A trio of oversized Canada geese, each with two hissing heads. Something that appears to be a cross between a walrus and a snapping turtle. There's even a giant, lumbering Bigfoot. So it's true: they *do* exist!

But you don't give it any more thought. You bolt

through the open door, and then use your entire body weight to close it. The door is taking a long time to swing back into position. You see the animals coming towards the narrowing gap, and—

CLUNK. It slams into place.

You lift the handle, and the light above the door shifts from green to red.

That guard's still in there, but he probably knows how to get out. Maybe you've bought yourself a little time, but how much?

You turn and run back down the corridor. You're not out of this place yet, but you're safe for now.

00:00

You survived! There are ten other ways to escape the danger— try to find them all!

You're no monster. Even though it might be the biggest mistake you'll ever make, you shakily step closer to the sasquatch's table. Instead of raging at you from its restraints, the sasquatch looks at you peacefully. "Grrrrngl," it says.

Phew! You cough away the worst breath and B.O. you've ever smelled. If you both make it out of here alive, you hope that the sasquatch finds itself a good shower!

"Just hold still," you tell the sasquatch, as you inch the scalpel closer. You're worried that the sasquatch is going to freak out when it sees the metal blade, but amazingly it holds still. It even shifts its wrist out of the way so that you can squeeze the blade in closer.

You saw the blade back and forth against the first restraint, and—

POP! Its hairy hand springs out of the strap.

"Grrnnnrggr?" the sasquatch asks. Yes, *asks*, you decide. It uses its newly free hand to point to the other strap holding it prisoner.

"Please don't make me regret this," you say, and finish cutting the sasquatch loose.

You expect the sasquatch to jump up and race away. Instead, it carefully slides off the table and moves stealthily across the room.

By the time it reaches the door, you're still frozen on the spot. It turns to you and shrugs its shoulders. "Grrrng!" it blurts at you, jabbing a hairy finger your way.

"You want me to follow you?"

"Grrrrngngr," it says.

"I'll take that as a yes," you return. Right now, it's the only living creature around here that you trust.

You watch in amazement as the animal opens the door to the room, and then peers out into a long, dark hallway.

The sasquatch turns back to you and puts a hairy finger to your lips. You try really hard not to choke on the nauseous smell. But you get its drift: *Keep quiet.*

And that's exactly what you do.

You'd think that a creature nicknamed "Bigfoot" would be prone to stomping about like an elephant, but the sasquatch is surprisingly nimble on its feet, barely making a sound. You, meanwhile, practically have to sprint to keep up with the beast.

It does seem to know where it's going. The sasquatch takes a fork in the tunnels. You're definitely in some kind of underground base. Heavy metal doors that look like they belong in a submarine line the corridors.

Surprisingly, the base is nearly empty.

Another left, then a right.

Soon you're outside a doorway with a stairway symbol marked above it. The sasquatch pulls the handle, and sure enough, there's a huge metal stairway stretching up and down as far as you can see.

"Grrnnnngl!"

You don't need to be told twice.

Now you're running with the sasquatch up the staircase, out the door and into daylight.

How did the sasquatch know the way? Has it been here before?

Your mind is full of questions, but you know the sasquatch is unlikely to answer them. It stares at you and makes a gesture that almost looks like a high-five. You're not sure if you should smack its hand or not. Instead you just break into a silly grin. "Thanks, Sasquatch," you say. "I owe you one!"

"Grrngrrrr!" And with that the sasquatch turns and disappears into the thickening forest. You take a few deep breaths as the majestic animal vanishes.

You're still stuck out here, but you've got a head start on those guards, and with luck, you might even find your friends.

For the first time, you get the feeling that there's someone—or something—looking out for you in the woods.

00:00

You survived! There are ten other ways to escape the danger— try to find them all!

02:50

You open the door and enter a darkened room.

There are no windows. No lights. No furniture of any kind. You're about to turn around and head back out when the door slams shut. You try the handle, but it's locked.

"No!" you blurt. You try again. It doesn't budge.

Great. How are you going to get out of here now?

You are answered with a nerve-racking silence.

It's just you and your quick breathing. Then . . .

The far wall begins to glow and pulse with colours. They shift from reds to blues to greens to shades you've never seen before. It's hypnotic. You can't tear your eyes away from it.

What. Is. This. Place? John said something about unbelievable experiments, didn't he? Is this part of one?

It's not just the sights that are making your mind spin, but also the sounds. A deep thrum that's both mechanical and organic emanates from the wall.

The colours draw you closer to the wall. You reach out your hand to touch it. But the wall is not solid. Your hand passes right through it.

Everything you know tells you to stop, to run back, but instead you follow some kind of ancient instinct buried deep inside you. You push your body into the gelatinous material that forms the wall.

The pulse of sound fills your ears, your entire body, as you press into the substance.

The room swallows you . . .

. . .

. . .

Darkness.

You're moving now.

Can't feel any legs.

Or arms.

Can't breathe, but you're alive.

Moving through liquid.

You open and close your mouth.

Feel the water flow past you, move through you.

Hungry.

Move to the surface.

Yes, the water has a surface. You break it.

In the distance, you make out the trees, mountains.

Your brain registers these as objects, but they are not safe anymore. You must stay in the water forever. You need it to survive.

That wall you passed through? It's changed you. Turned you into a creature of the deep, dark waters.

THE END.

To try again, go back to page 50.

03:09

Save life! Get to ground!

That's what makes you do something crazy, like throw all of your weight to one side of the bar.

The glider veers sharply, turning so fast and hard that you're facing sideways.

"What are you doing? Are you nuts?" Prisha shouts. She grabs at you to regain control of the glider, maybe even to throw you off it.

No way. You're not going down without a fight. You squeeze the bar even harder, sending the glider spinning. No time to rethink this one. You push closer and closer to the mountainside, hoping that the landing won't kill you as surely as those guards will.

SMASH! The glider crunches into a pine tree.

The sudden stop sends you reeling. You let go of the bar, and for a second, you're in mid-air.

Then, *oof!* You're flung stomach first into one of the thick branches. It knocks the wind out of you, but you double over and grip the branch tightly.

You hang there, legs dangling, for what seems like forever. You gulp in a few breaths, and then look up.

Prisha's tangled in the remains of her hang-glider. There's a gash on her forehead, and for a second, you fear the worst. But then you see her chest rising and falling. She's just unconscious.

Thankfully the trees here are so thick with branches that you're able to manoeuvre down them.

Then you spot something that makes your eyes light up.

Prisha's radio. You scoop it up and fiddle with the buttons. It still works.

You can hear the helicopter searching for you and Prisha. They'll probably spot the glider soon, but you're far enough away from the base that it'll take the guards a long time to catch up with you on foot. And you're deep enough in the woods that the chopper can't land easily. You've bought yourself some time.

As for Prisha? You notice her stirring. She looks around, senses how high she is, and begins to panic.

"What have you done?" Prisha mutters.

"No, it's more like—what are you going to do now? Those guards aren't going to wait around forever. And neither am I." Clutching the radio, you turn away.

"Get back here!" she shouts. "We're better together than alone!"

Nah, you think. Right now, you've got no one you can trust but yourself. And all you can think is one thing: *Run!*

00:00

You survived! There are ten other ways to escape the danger— try to find them all!

03:09

You're whooshing through the sky with no lifeline, in the company of someone who seems to have more skills than James Bond. You bet your booties you're going to shut up and do what she says.

"How are we going to shake that helicopter?" you ask.

"Like I said, I've got everything covered. You just enjoy the view," she says.

The view? Can't Prisha tell how terrified of heights you are? "The view is going to make me spew!"

"Then it's a good thing you're below me. Now look over there!"

Where? She taps you on the head and you look up. Prisha's pointing into the distance.

You squint to see what she's getting at. There, on one of the mountains in the distance, is a dusty old road that leads into a tunnel. And waiting in the tunnel, flashing its headlights in some kind of Morse code, is a truck.

Prisha's people!

You whip your head back around. You want to give her a massive thumbs-up, but letting go of the bar is not on your to-do list at the moment. Instead, you wink. Or, you're about to, but the helicopter's suddenly bearing down on you.

It's so close that you can see right into the cockpit. The pilot's got a sinister smile on his face. Meanwhile, the co-pilot is leaning out of the doorway, with one foot on the landing skid. He's aiming a laser right at you.

ZAP! The skin of the glider sizzles.

ZAP! ZAP!

You feel the glider drop sharply.

"We're gonna crash!" you shout.

"Easy," Prisha says, but her voice is shaky.

You look down. You're still high above the canyon. The river below is just a blue ribbon, and the jagged boulders look like pebbles—for now.

ZAP! ZAP!

Prisha leans left, then right. You're nearly thrown from the glider, but when you look at the mountain, it's almost as close as the helicopter. You're coming in fast now—too fast.

You feel something slap against your head, and you see the buckles and straps of the harness swinging in the air.

"What the—"

"Get ready to jump!"

"What?"

"It's a dirt road," Prisha says. "Just tuck and roll on my word."

"What word?"

"NOW!"

You let go. Tuck and roll. The mountain rushes at you.

More like drop and splat. You slam against the ground, first stomach, then chin, then—

SMASH! You lie in agony on the ground. You're dead, or dying. You're sure of it.

Then you open your eyes.

A hand reaches across your field of vision. You're pulled away from the road. You look up.

"Get up!" Prisha coughs. She grabs hold of you and yanks you into the tunnel.

Clouds of dust swirl around you. You're barely standing, on knees wobbly as Jell-O. You don't even feel it as you lumber over to the truck. The door is flung open, and you're flung inside. You slam against the back seat. Prisha slams into you. The driver floors it. The truck spins around and speeds through the tunnel.

Darkness swallows you up.

You take a few deep breaths and look over to see Prisha doing the same.

Then, looking at you, she cracks a crazed smile. "You really messed up this job," she says, "but you've got guts."

"Huh?"

"I can tell you're going to make an excellent operative," she says as the truck blazes off, carrying you who-knows-where.

THE END.

To try again, go back to page 12.

06:16

You veer left and end up in another long corridor. This one curves around so much you can't see where it terminates. It looks just like the last corridor, except midway down the hall, over one of the doors . . .

. . . is the *green* light!

Cautiously, you move towards the door, grip the handle, and give it a tug. The door squeals open a sliver, and you have to shoulder your weight against it to open it fully. You stumble into a much larger room, and your eyes go wide.

There's medical equipment covering tabletops and mounted to the ceiling. Some of the tables are just metal slabs over sewer-like grates in the floor. There are pools of red liquid below.

You struggle to take it all in.

Again you ask yourself: *What* is *this place?*

It takes a few moments for your gaze to move from the mass of spooky equipment to the outer edges of the room. That's when your eyes grow even wider.

A series of doors and large windows take up the perimeter of the room. Some of the windows are darkened, but others are lit. It seems each looks into a separate room.

Out of the corner of your eye you sense movement coming from one of them, and you edge closer.

Slowly, you approach the window from an angle. You strain to get a better look at what's in the room.

It appears empty—except for gouges in the wall, as if someone has been trying to claw his or her way out.

You move even closer, trying to see just a little more, and—

BAM!

A big, hairy claw slams against the glass. You jump back, landing firmly on your butt. It must be super thick glass, because a claw that big would have shattered any ordinary windowpane.

What . . . the . . . ?

The thing trapped in the room moves directly into your field of vision, and you nearly let out a scream.

It's a bear.

At least, it's part bear.

Because mounted onto its head is a pair of jagged antlers, like you'd normally see on a moose. Only they're far spikier than a moose's antlers. More like a fusion of antler and cactus spike.

As the creature starts to growl, you hear other animal sounds from around the room. Clicks and cries and whinnies and buzzes.

What is going on in this place?

You back away from the bear-thing's enclosure,

catching sight of a scaly tail on its back end.

You spot another creature behind a different window. This one looks part beaver, on account of the giant tail and furry body. But instead of rodent-like teeth, this beaver has a giant pair of sabre-toothed tiger fangs. And it's scuttling across the floor on giant crab legs.

Yikes. You wouldn't want that thing to get out of its room.

BLANG! BLANG! BLANG! BLANG!

Oh no.

Before you can turn and run back into the hallway, you hear heavy footsteps storming towards you. Great.

You quickly duck behind one of the surgical tables, nearly slipping in a filmy residue on the floor.

Suddenly, an armed guard bursts into the room.

"I know you're in here," he says.

You want to stand up and explain everything that's happened, but this guy doesn't look like he wants to hear what you have to say. Plus, you have the feeling you've seen more than you should have.

On the upside, you still haven't been spotted. You frantically twist your head, looking for a means of escape, or a weapon.

That's when you notice that the cell right behind you is dark. Maybe it's empty?

You can't get past this guard just yet. But if you

could open the cell door . . . you might be able to hide in there.

Then you turn the other way, and you notice a big red button on a control panel a few paces away. When you strain your eyes, you see *EMERGENCY RELEASE* written in block letters just above it.

Ooh, that's a very tempting button. You could release these crazy animals to distract the guard and make your escape.

Choices, choices . . .

If you open the door to the darkened cell and duck inside, turn to page 76.

If you press the BIG RED BUTTON and make a break for it, turn to page 57.

06:16

The fewer twists and turns you take, the less likely you are to get lost. At some point you're going to need to get out of here, and who knows how big this place is.

But first you want to know where Prisha's going. As you push deeper down the corridor, you hear mechanical sounds. A clink of machinery and a hum of fans in the distance. Looking up, you notice wires and pipes running all the way down the corridor, branching off behind various closed doors.

You spy Ethernet cables mixed into the tightly packed cords. You wonder if they lead to computers. If you can get online, maybe you can get help.

You pick up the pace and follow the ever-thickening series of cables to a door at the end of the hallway. There's no light above it at all, and it's ajar.

You stop, look over your shoulder to make sure you haven't been followed, and peer inside. Is Prisha here? Or was she here already? The room is only half-lit, but it's full of computers—and no sign of Prisha. Some of them are desktops, but most are long computer banks, like in old spy movies. There are dozens of monitors, many showing what looks like security cam footage.

It's clearly not where these guys play video games.

The room looks empty, so you decide to slip inside the nerve centre of the compound.

Immediately, you spy your live image on one of the larger monitors. You move your hand up and down, and the image does the same. Great—you're being watched. *Better move quickly*, you think. You pace along a row of computers. There are scores of images on the monitors, seemingly from every security camera in the joint.

You look at one bank of computers with a few large buttons and a pair of keys slotted into it. Then you spot *SELF-DESTRUCT* written in bold letters above the keys. There's a bunch of small writing below it.

Self-destruct? What is this place, and why would it have a crazy self-destruct switch? Plus who would leave the keys in the switch?

A moment later you understand why nobody's here: On one monitor, you see Prisha. She's with a gaggle of armed guards. Two hold her by the arms, and more surround her.

You can see her lips moving, and you turn the volume up on the monitor.

"What you're doing is monstrous," she says. She looks more angry than frightened. "You're taking those animals, turning them into weapons. Don't you have any conscience?"

"You've trespassed into a top-secret facility," one of

the guards says matter-of-factly. "You will be prosecuted to the full extent of the law."

"Or maybe you won't," another chimes in.

"What do you mean?"

"You could just . . . disappear," one of the guards states. "Much easier to deal with."

"We could wipe the video footage of her entry," another suggests.

You see Prisha's expression shift to worry. And then you gulp. Wiping the footage means they'll be heading back here.

You can't just let them get away with this. But you're no match for all those guards.

Or are you?

You could set the self-destruct switch. That would get everybody freaked out and escaping for their lives, and give Prisha a chance to get out too. You'd have to make a break for it yourself. It would be effective, but super risky.

You could also try to go online and contact the police, then lay low until they come to investigate.

If you set the self-destruct sequence, turn to page 134.
If you contact the police, turn to page 138.

01:35

Y ou're no match for this guard, especially if he's armed. Slowly, carefully, you reach back for the door. You keep your eyes glued to the guard as he searches the laboratory. He doesn't look when the door squeaks ever so slightly. You try to duck inside, but you need to open the door a little bit more. Just enough to slip through.

There. You've done it! You don't close the door all the way. The less movement and noise you make, the better.

You don't hear any growling, and there's no animal smell in here. The room is empty, so you sit and wait.

Except then you hear a high-pitched whine by your ear.

Ack! Mosquito. You feel it pinch your neck and give it a slap. Another buzz. Another mosquito.

Slap! Slap!

What are they doing in here?

You begin to feel itchy pricks all over your exposed skin: arms, legs—it's not like you went on a canoe trip wearing jeans and a long-sleeved shirt.

You feel an irresistible urge to keep scratching. The more you slap at your skin, the more insects you feel on your hands, which are getting increasingly wet.

The door slams shut. A light blazes on above you, and your heart leaps into your throat.

Through the window, you see the guard watching you. He's got you trapped, and the look on his face is a mixture of satisfaction and horror.

You look around and understand. The room is full of mosquitoes. They're covering the walls, swarming in small clouds.

They're a little bigger than normal, but there are so many of them. They're covering your body. Every bit of skin is carpeted in a layer of buzzing insects. You watch as they suck your blood, each mosquito growing bigger and bigger. Soon the itching is replaced with light-headedness. You're losing too much blood, too quickly.

You stagger towards the doorway, but pinpricks of black cloud your vision.

One step. Two steps. You're down on the floor.

You reach for the door. But your arm doesn't even look like your arm anymore. Just an outstretched limb covered in a layer of wriggling, buzzing mosquitoes. They've got your blood, you think.

But you can't think too clearly.

Too light-headed. Your mind swims in itchy darkness.

You try to keep your eyes open, but all you see are wings, and then you feel the pinch of mosquitoes around your eyes, and—

THE END.

To try again, go back to page 25.

08:22

You follow John as he moves up the mountainside, heading away from the valley and towards a clearing in the woods. Phew. Maybe he doesn't want you jumping off that crazy cliff after all. Prisha might be good at that sort of thing, but you're not!

You reach the clearing, and—

You're standing in front of a massive grate. You peer over the edge and down—way down—into the darkness below.

A gust of hot, stale air blows in your face, tossing your hair around.

Oh man, what is John up to?

He doesn't talk to you. He's too busy fiddling with the chains holding the grate in place. He pulls his weird laser from its holster. An intense red beam cuts through the metal chains like they're made of balsa wood.

Snap!

Finally, John looks at you. "Come help me with this."

He locks his fingers into a portion of the metal grate and heaves back on it. You join in, although you've got arms like string beans. Both of you grunt and pull with all of your might, and the grate slowly squeals open.

Panting for breath, you watch as John starts to fiddle

with the cord he had in that backpack. At first, you wonder if it's a bungee cord, but no—it's more like a thick wire tethered to a spool and a harness rig that John is now assembling. He wraps one end of the wire around a solid-looking tree trunk and then fishes around in the backpack for a harness.

You stand there in disbelief, looking from him to the deep pit below.

"Okay," John says at last. "We're ready."

He hands you the harness.

"Our reconnaissance is state of the art," he says. "We've calculated the exact depth of the chamber. The cord will give you a few metres to manoeuvre around the cooling fan."

"Cooling fan?"

"Yes, watch the blades. They're sharp, and you're going down headfirst. If you miss your mark, you'll wind up decapitated."

"Oh," you say.

"After your jump, you'll find a doorway near the bottom. Go through the door and down the corridor."

"Right," you say, trying to take in these instructions.

"You can't miss the breaker," John says. "Flip it off, and the power will be cut to the entire complex. That'll give our operatives a chance to infiltrate more readily. You'll just need to double back to the cord."

Before you can argue, or even tell him that it's all

a big mistake and that you're not Prisha, he's begun to strap you into the harness. Dang! Running away was the only other option you had, and now that's gone too.

"I'll be waiting for you here," John says. "Once you're back at the cord, give it a tug and I'll pull you up."

"Uhhh," you say, and then you catch John staring at you strangely. "Sounds like a blast!"

You look away from John's steely gaze and glance over the edge of the chamber. Your heart is in your throat.

You take some deep breaths.

You can do this. People bungee jump all the time. This can't be that different from that, right?

Do this.

Now.

And you jump.

You gasp as solid ground falls away and you are swallowed by darkness. Wind whips through your hair and screams in your ears.

And . . .

. . . you come to a standstill.

. . . and you're still screaming, until you realize . . .

YOU ARE NOT DEAD.

Phew! John sure knew what he was talking about when he said he'd calculated the depth of this chamber. Because you are hanging upside down over the slowly spinning blades. *Wow, that fan is big!* Below the giant fan is a chute that must lead to the heat exchanger or something. You definitely don't want to fall down there. Between the blades and the chute, you'll either be cooked or turned into mincemeat. But what's your other option?

You spy a ledge with an open door on the wall of the chamber. That must be where you're meant to go.

Oh, great. You're going to need to swing yourself over there, catch hold of the door, and then untie yourself.

But you can't really do the best job of swinging while you're upside down, can you? The blood is rushing to your head and your field of vision is already getting all cloudy. You don't want to pass out down here.

It might be easier to untie yourself first so you can use your legs to pump your body back and forth. But maybe you should keep the cord attached to the harness until you're back on solid ground.

If you stay upside down and keep the cord attached, turn to page 82.
If you try untying yourself, turn to page 83.

05:06

You can't risk falling down, and untying yourself now is just asking for trouble. Maybe your arms are like tiny noodles, but you've got guts!

You start swinging yourself back and forth, back and forth.

Sure enough, you get a rhythm going, and your body moves with each swing. As you gain momentum, the door comes closer and closer—almost within reach—and then . . .

"Got it!" you blurt. You take hold of the door's long handle with one hand and you use your free hand to release the cord from around your feet.

As gravity drops you, you clutch the door handle and lower yourself onto the ledge.

Phew.

Now, to find that breaker. John said something about it being down a corridor, didn't he? Piece of cake.

Wait. There's another doorway here.

What *did* John say? Down a corridor? Is this the right one? But why is there a doorway here? And where does it lead? Were you supposed to go through it first?

If you go through the door, turn to page 62.
If you go down the corridor, turn to page 42.

05:06

no way are you going to make it to that door while hanging upside down. You're going to have to untie yourself first. You start fiddling with the Velcro straps harnessing you to the rope, giving them a pull, and—

"WAAAAAGH!"

You fall.

Down.

Fast.

You scream, watching the fan blades come right past your head, but you slip through a gap between the blades and fall onto the smaller metal chute below. It curves downward, taking you with it like you're in an enclosed slide.

Still screaming, you can't do anything until gravity does its part first. Soon enough, the vent bottoms out and you find yourself in a small metal chamber that opens into a tunnel.

It's still part of the exhaust vent, only . . .

Only there's a small doorway up ahead. You could try taking that. Or you could work your way along the tunnel and look for another way out.

If you go through the door, turn to page 62.
If you keep heading down the tunnel, turn to page 88.

Using the mirror as your guide, you gently move your hand over to the blade.

It pricks your exposed skin, drawing forth a bubble of blood.

Careful, you remind yourself. You try again.

This time, the scalpel cuts into the leather strap binding you to the table. You begin to wiggle your wrist back and forth, back and forth.

The more you wriggle, the looser the strap gets. You keep up the momentum, until—*pop!* Your wrist breaks free of the strap.

Wasting no time, you reach for the scalpel with your free hand and begin sawing your way out of the other straps. First your other hand, then your ankles. All the while you sneak glances at the sasquatch. It's been watching you quietly this whole time. It seems to sense that keeping a low profile is the best strategy—or is that all in your head? You can't possibly read the emotions of a giant sasquatch, can you?

"Yes!" you say to yourself as you move your legs. You're free.

Carefully, you slide off the operating table and onto

the cold floor. Thank goodness you've still got your shoes and your clothes on!

Scalpel in hand, you sneak through the room. It's cluttered with all kinds of medical equipment. Monitors bleep and ping around you, bringing back memories of the time you had your appendix removed.

Who knows what kind of crazy surgery these guys were planning for you, but you're getting out of here.

"Grrrrng," the sasquatch grunts.

You turn and look at it. The hairy giant is still strapped to the table. Your eyes meet its eyes. This is no thought-less animal, you realize. You can read the expressions on its face: pain, fear and pleading.

You could set this poor creature free, but there's no telling what it might do. It's a wild animal, and strong enough to crack your spine like a twig.

If you cut the sasquatch free, turn to page 59.

If you make an escape on your own, turn to page 86.

??:??

"**G**rrngrr!" the sasquatch pleads, whimpering like a little kid.

"I'm sorry," you say. You can't believe you're apologizing to this creature, but you have no idea what it's capable of. It could turn on you and smash you to pieces.

Ignoring its pained cries, you sneak across the room and reach a doorway at the back.

Click.

Around you, lights in the room flick on.

No!

Shoes click against floor, and then an older man appears. He's wearing a white lab coat and his hands are squeezed into a pair of latex gloves.

He moves past the sasquatch and over to you. Saying nothing, he grabs you by the arm and squeezes it firmly enough that you yelp. Then he forces you into a set of restraints.

"What are you doing to me?" you ask.

"I suppose there's no use keeping information from you," the man says. "I dare say you won't be able to use it."

You gulp. "You're going to kill me?"

The man cracks a smile. "*Kill* you? Good heavens, no.

If we wanted to do that, you wouldn't be in this room, would you? What do you think this place is? A mortuary?"

"Then where am I?"

"Conversion room," the man says. He's moving past you to the tray of surgical equipment. He takes a needle and then reaches to a tray out of view, grabs a vial of clear liquid, and plunges the needle into it. Your heart skips a beat.

"Conversion?"

"Well, more like hybridization," he says. "Gene-splicing, molecule-splitting." He pulls the needle out of the vial, squeezes a few drops of liquid from it, and then turns back to you. "But don't worry. I don't intend to cause any more pain than necessary."

You struggle against the restraints, but there's no hope. No chance.

You wince as the needle jabs your arm and he pushes down on the plunger. You feel a hot liquid pulse through your veins.

A moment later, your head grows woozy. You hear his voice, but his words echo dreamily. "You're becoming something unique. We need human recruits for this kind of work. Luckily for us, you came to the right place, at the right time . . ."

Then, blackness.

Turn to page 108.

02:50

You continue down the tunnel. It's dark and stuffy, but if you're careful you might find another way out of this exhaust system, then work your way out of this crazy complex.

Up ahead, you notice a fork in the tunnel. And right at the intersection is a panel with various high-tech equipment: buttons, monitors and flashing lights.

Could this be what John was talking about?

You don't see any switch. And John didn't say anything about going through the blades of the fan. He wanted you to go down a corridor, probably through that doorway above the fan. But what if that led down here?

There's only one way to find out, so you move closer to the panel.

As you do, a loud alarm begins to sound.

The chamber is bathed in ominous red light.

The digital panel flashes to life. It just says *INTRUDER.*

"No," you say. You turn around to escape through the door you just passed, but—

The pressure in the tunnel changes.

The whole ventilation shaft vibrates and hums with energy, and you feel a massive pull against your body.

The fan! It's on!

You try to grip the walls, but they're smooth as glass.

And then, *FOOM!* You're flying back up the chute, the way you came . . .

Only now the spinning blades of the fan are at full speed and you're headed right towards them.

THE END.

To try again, go back to page 50.

00:58

An alarm echoes through the valley. You've been spotted! You can't see the top of the dam from where you are, but you hear footsteps running towards you. You look at the bomb. There are only seconds left.

"You down there!" a gruff voice barks. "Put your hands up!"

You look up to see five or six silhouettes.

"You don't understand," you call up, "there's a b—"

"Hands up, if you know what's good for you!"

No time to explain. You glance at the timer. Less than three minutes, so about fifteen seconds in real time . . .

You stand up and cautiously raise your hands. *Easy does it*, you tell yourself.

And then, mustering up all of your muscle power, you kick the bomb off the ledge, hoping that you've got enough time.

Somebody notices the falling object.

"Is that a—"

BOOM!

The hot blast knocks you back on the ledge. The ground around you shakes and shudders.

And then the shaking subsides.

You crawl to the edge of the ledge.

There's no damage to the dam. Everything's safe!

You breathe a short sigh of relief. You flip back over and take a better look at the guards peering down at you. As you squint, you can make out the form of Prisha. She's got her hands over her head, guards flanking her sides, a defeated look on her face.

You've got a lot of explaining to do, but man, oh man: Best. Kick. *Ever!*

00:00

You survived! There are ten other ways to escape the danger— try to find them all!

03:19

You've come this far with your crazy stunts, and you're not about to stop now.

Clutching the Jet Ski's handles, you grit your teeth and brace for the jump of your life.

You watch as the world spins around you. Down is up. Up is down. The deep blue water below you is replaced with an azure-blue sky and the blazing bulb of the sun. The centrifugal force of the whirling Jet Ski holds you in place.

OMG. This is amazing! You're doing it. You're going to pull a complete 360 during a high-speed chase. You're amazing! You're the champ!

You're—

About to land headfirst in open water at a dangerously high speed.

Worst. Fail. Ever.

SPLAT!

THE END.

To try again, go back to page 25.

03:19

nstinct tells you to bail on the Jet Ski.

You let go.

And scream.

You're flung through the air, your arms and legs thrashing. Then—

SPLASH!

You plunge deep into the frigid water. You sink like a stone. You're about to surface, but you look up through the murky lake to see the Jet Ski land just above you. You dive back down instead.

Phew, that was close!

When you're sure that the Jet Ski is no longer a danger—and when you're just about to run out of breath—you swim back to the surface and pop up beside the Jet Ski.

From your vantage point you can see Prisha farther down the lake, but you're pretty sure she can't see you.

Prisha looks over her shoulder, turns her Jet Ski around, and presses onward. You dog-paddle for a moment, but time's running out if you want to make your move.

If you get back on your Jet Ski and follow Prisha, turn to page 28.

If you try to swim to shore, turn to page 94.

02:21

Enough with Prisha!

You survived the crash into the water. The edge of the lake isn't too far away. You can totally swim this: it's only a few pool lengths from where you are.

You begin to swim across the lake, but the harder you kick, the farther away the shore seems. It doesn't make sense.

Then, from behind, you hear splashing.

You turn and see the remains of the dam come crumbling down. Smoke and clouds of crushed concrete billow into the air around you.

But now that you're treading water, you notice that you're moving closer and closer to the dam.

No!

Water is rushing through the area that had been dammed. But some of the structure is still there, and all of the water is being funnelled through a single massive hole in the dam.

You've been in enough wading pools to know that a ton of water and a small drain can mean only one thing: WHIRLPOOL!

You turn around and feverishly paddle towards the shore, but now you're speeding away from it instead.

You feel the undertow grip your legs and hurl you into the whirlpool. Bits of debris swirl around you. Your Jet Ski bobs up and down, trying its best to stay afloat, but then—*PLOP!*—it suddenly shoots down the dark eye of the maelstrom and disappears. Round and round you go. You scream for help, but Prisha's way downstream at this point.

All you can do is stare in horrified wonder as the vortex gets closer and closer.

You open your mouth for one last scream, but all that comes out is . . .

Gurglegurglegurglegurgle—

THE END.

To try again, go back to page 25.

14:25

You put your arms out to stop yourself from falling, but it's no good. You clench your teeth, and—

An arm shoots out, slapping you across your rib cage and flinging you back to solid ground. You land in a heap on the rocks. Prisha stands over you, shaking her head. Man, she's strong.

"Look before you leap, eh?"

Prisha pulls you back to your feet. You peer over the edge.

Below, a massive dam stretches across a valley, between this mountain and another. It's an immense curved concrete wall, like the Hoover Dam in the US. On one side of the dam is a large blue lake, and on the other side is a river winding through the valley.

"This used to be pristine wilderness," Prisha says disgustedly. "That lake has flooded acres of land. But those animal experiments are even worse. We're going to get down there and sabotage the facility." She says it so matter-of-factly that a shiver runs down your spine.

"What about the people in there?"

"It's just a skeleton crew," Prisha insists. "We'll . . . give them a warning first."

Then Prisha looks past you and her eyes light up. "A-ha!"

A few paces away, there's a backpack sitting at the edge of the woods. You follow her over. She bends down and unzips it so that you can see what's inside: several blocks wrapped together, with a timer affixed on top. A bomb!

Whoever Prisha says she is, this is going too far, even if she claims to have her reasons. You can't let this go.

The bomb doesn't appear to be primed yet. If you act quickly, there's a chance you can grind this operation to a halt.

If you grab the bomb from Prisha, turn to page 98.

If you wait this out and see what Prisha's plans are, turn to page 100.

13:48

You lunge forward, snatch the backpack out of Prisha's hands, and pivot towards the edge of the cliff.

"Bombs away!" you cry. With all your might, you toss the backpack—bomb and all—over the edge of the mountain. Hopefully it lands where you want it to—smack dab in the middle of the lake, away from the actual dam. You were never that great at shot put, though.

"You idiot!" Prisha screams, watching the bomb drop. "You've ruined everything!"

"What? The timer isn't on. It's not gonna blow. It's totally fine," you say smugly. "Isn't it?"

"It's chock full of explosives and detonators—"

BOOOOOM!

A huge geyser erupts from the lake.

"Oh," you say, watching the cloud of vapour dissipate into the air around you. You wait for any signs of structural damage to the dam, but everything seems A-okay. "Direct hit. No people harmed. Nice try, Prisha!"

She just motions to the base below.

On cue, alarms start ringing out.

"Riiiiiiight," you say. It's possible you didn't think this one all the way through. As the alarms blare, a doorway on top of the base flings open and guards spill out. It takes them only a few moments to spy you on the clifftop and start firing giant laser beams in your direction.

"Whoa!" you exclaim. "Laser guns! Is this base in the future or something?"

The ground before you explodes into clouds of dust. You double back quickly, but Prisha is already scrambling through the woods. It's no wonder why—a moment later you hear the whooshing blades of helicopters coming closer. Some skeleton crew this turned out to be!

As you race after Prisha, your mind whirls and you try to sort out what the heck is going on around here. *You* were the one who stopped her from blowing the base up. She was bent on causing total destruction. Maybe following her isn't so smart. Maybe you just need to lay low.

If you wait things out, turn to page 102.

If you follow Prisha back into the woods, turn to page 104.

13:48

Prisha digs deeper into the backpack and pulls out a few small metal cylinders. She carefully places them into the blocks, then hits a button on the timer panel until a clock lights up. She's so preoccupied with her work that it takes a second before she remembers she's not alone.

"Oh," she remarks, looking at you, and then at the bomb. "You've probably got some questions."

Now that Prisha's activated a bomb, it's not the time to try pressing your luck.

"You obviously know your way around explosives," you say as coolly as you can. "Did they teach you that in canoe tripper school?"

She takes it as a joke and gives you a little smirk. "It was the perfect cover," she insists. "A single operative nearing the complex would be noticed and tracked. But a group of kids? Nothing to worry about. What harm could kids do?"

What harm could kids do? *Plenty*, you think to yourself. You just need to find a good time and place to get rid of this bomb and put Prisha in her place.

"Clever," you say through gritted teeth.

"It is, isn't it?" She picks up the backpack and carefully

slips her arms through the straps. She then moves back towards the cliff. "And it worked. I pretended to get separated from the group. Chose a day that the complex was under lax security. And now we're going to put it out of commission."

You and Prisha are now standing at the edge of the mountain, looking down at the massive base below.

"We?" you ask. "I don't know anything about bombs."

How are you going to climb down there with her? More importantly, how are you going to stop her?

"You don't need to. You've got a very important role to play."

"What's that?" you ask.

"*You're* the decoy," she says.

"Wha—"

Before you can finish your thought, you feel a sudden push. Your body pitches forward. You throw out your arms to catch something—anything—to break your fall.

There's nothing. Just air.

You watch the face of the mountain rush past as you hurtle towards the ground below. Prisha saved you all right, you realize. Saved you for *this*.

THE END.
To try again, go back to page 12.

07:17

You stop running and catch your breath. It comes in jagged spurts that stab at your lungs like daggers. A thick film of sweat pastes your clothes to your back. Prisha doesn't even look back to see if you're keeping pace with her. You watch her disappear into the tangle of branches until she's just a blur in the distance. You shake your head. Good riddance!

You're on your own, but not for long. The roar of the approaching helicopter gets even louder.

You crane your head skyward. The helicopter is bearing down on you. Trees bend and sway as it draws closer.

You duck and sprint through the forest.

Putting your hands out, you block the branches and sticks coming your way.

Maybe you should have stayed with Prisha after all. Up ahead, you spot a blur of movement in the forest. "Prisha!" you shout. "Wait up!"

Prisha stops, whirls around, and looks at you.

It's tall, it's dark. It's not Prisha.

You stand there, dumbfounded. No. It's impossible.

But it's just like you've seen on TV and the internet a gazillion times. You're staring at a sasquatch!

It looks at you. Then, even more impossibly, it motions for you to follow it.

"Huh?"

You blink, and then it's gone. Maybe it was all your imagination.

Above, the helicopter grows even closer. Cripes! You've been spotted.

Gusts of wind from the spinning rotors knock you off your feet. You struggle to get up, but already you can see armed guards pushing through the forest around you.

You raise your hands to show these guys that you mean them no harm. "It's okay!" you scream, but your voice is drowned out by the chopper. "I'm not with her! It's all a horrible mistake!"

But they don't lower their guns.

The men push forward. You gulp. This isn't what you planned.

One of them calls out to the guard closest to you. He in turn lowers his gun—

Phew.

—only to load some kind of dart into it. He points it right at you.

Your stomach drops. "No!" you scream.

He pulls the trigger.

Turn to page 35.

07:17

Prisha had a bomb, but these guards have lasers.

"Hurry up, if you know what's good for you," Prisha urges. "Those guards won't let you out of here in one piece!"

You don't need to be told twice.

You scramble after her. If you thought sneaking through the forest was treacherous, running blindly through the woods is just torture. Jagged branches and thorns lash at any exposed skin with such speed you'd think you were the main ingredient in a Ginsu knife infomercial.

You wince at the pain, but there's no time to slow down. Trees explode around you as lasers hit them.

Follow Prisha. You say it in your head over and over to drown out everything else.

Follow Prisha. Follow Prisha. Follow Prisha. Follow—

You slide to a halt. There she is, at a clearing in the forest. It takes you a second to realize two things: 1) you and Prisha are at the edge of the tallest cliff you've ever seen, and 2) there's a hang-glider waiting for you.

Prisha wastes no time strapping herself into the harness.

"What is going on here?" you wheeze.

Shouts ring out in the woods. Those guards are getting closer by the second.

"Let's go," Prisha snaps. "Before I change my mind."

The roar of the helicopter gets closer. No time to argue about your intense fear of heights. You scurry over and look for extra harnesses. There are none.

"Yup," Prisha says, motioning to the big bar across the width of the glider. "This baby was designed for one, and one only. You're just going to have to hang on for dear life."

She grabs you and pushes off the edge of the cliff. You watch the ground rush away. It's replaced by a dizzying view of the chasm below. Your scream is drowned out by the sound of the chopper.

Of course you've been spotted. You're in a brightly coloured hang-glider.

Prisha leans sharply to the left, and the whole glider veers wildly. No wonder—you're sitting ducks up here, and if one of those lasers hits the glider, it won't stay airborne for long.

"Just hang on!" Prisha shouts. "I've got a plan!"

Now she's steering the glider downriver, zigzagging to stay out of range.

Maybe you're past the guards now, but you can't outrun a helicopter. Prisha's crazy. You've got to get out of the air, like, this instant!

If you take control of the steering, turn to page 64.

If you hang on for the ride, turn to page 66.

01:43

Y ou run.

You don't take more than a few steps when you hear a ping from John's box, and then hissing, snapping wolverines.

Don't look back, you think.

You look back.

Claws! Teeth!

"Eeeearrgh!" you scream.

But screaming doesn't stop the wolverines.

They're on your trail, and they're *fast*.

You can't outrun them, but maybe you can outclimb them. You dash towards the closest tree and hop onto a branch. You grab at any tree limb within reach. Some of them snap under your weight, but some hold, and you're able to hoist yourself up quickly.

"Take that, wolverines!" you blurt, and look down.

Oh no. Wolverines can climb. Like, they can climb fast. And better than you. Why don't they teach you this stuff in school?

Two of them are already pretty close to you. They're shimmying up the trunk, their beady eyes locked on you, snarling and frothing at the mouth. No wonder they named an X-Men character after these things!

You try to move farther up the tree. You're already high enough that a fall is going to break a bone, or six.

The height doesn't faze the wolverines at all.

"Help!" you scream. You look down at John, holding the remote. "They're going to kill me!"

John doesn't reply. He's watching the wolverines scramble up the tree after you.

"John, *please!*" you holler. The wolverines are now within reach. One of them slashes at you. You dodge the blow, and its claws tear grooves into the thick bark.

You're forced to scramble along one of the branches, away from the trunk.

The wolverines have you cornered.

You edge your way back, clinging to the branch for dear life. But the farther you get from the trunk, the thinner the branch gets, and soon it's bending under your weight.

You sway back and forth in the breeze, watching the closest wolverine slowly, intentionally climb towards you. You lock eyes with it, but it doesn't break your stare. It keeps its gaze fixed on you, snapping its teeth, edging closer, closer.

Then the wolverine lunges forward with its sharp claws, and this time you don't have any way to dodge the blow.

THE END.

To try again, go back to page 48.

??:??

Your eyes flutter open. You're not sure how long you've been asleep. You're definitely still in the same room. What had that crazy doctor called it? Conversion room?

Wherever you are, that guy is nowhere to be seen. Neither is the sasquatch. You're all alone.

Maybe you can pull your hands free from the straps and make a break for it.

You close your eyes and focus on wriggling your wrists against the restraints. No luck. They seem even tighter than they were before. You try twisting and turning. Urgh! It's really hard, although you feel like you've somehow gotten stronger. There's more energy in your body. Maybe there was something in that needle the doctor gave you.

"Come on!" you scream. Or rather, you *try* to scream. But your voice is drowned out by a low-pitched growl.

Cripes! That sasquatch has still got to be around here somewhere. You turn your head left, then right, but there's no sign of it.

But that sound is *definitely* coming from a sasquatch. Not that you're a sasquatch expert. Still, you pull at the straps binding you to the table. Now you look down at your arms and—

You scream.

Your hands. They're bigger. Hairier.

You scream again, but it's not a human scream. It's that same low-pitched roar you heard from the sasquatch.

No. It *can't* be!

Slowly, you turn your head so that you're staring into the mirror.

A sasquatch stares back at you.

You marvel at your reflection. You're wearing the shredded remains of your clothes, right down to your shoes, which hang in pieces from your shaggy oversized feet.

"Good morning," a voice booms from speakers somewhere in the room. It's that crazy old doctor.

"What have you done to me?" you yell, but your words come out as a series of guttural roars.

"Yes, yes," the doctor retorts. "I'm sure you're a tad confused. But I assure you this is all part of the procedure. What an amazing specimen you are!"

You struggle to shake free of your bonds, but you're secured to the table. Panic erupts. It's got to be some kind of nightmare, but no matter what you do, you can't wake up from it.

You're trapped in this place, and this body.

THE END.

To try again, go back to page 4.

04:38

So they've got some kind of salmon farm here. What's the big deal? You love salmon.

Using your paddle as a lever, you force open the heavy grate. You stare into the entrance, but you can't see all the way in, or how deep it goes.

"Hello?" you call out. You are greeted by an echo that hints at the sizeable chamber inside, and the sound of water lapping against the walls.

"Oh well," you shrug. "It's just a bunch of fish."

You paddle into the chamber. It's dark in here, kind of like being in a sea cave. The main source of light is outside.

You can't tell if there's a way to get into the main part of the dam complex from here, and it's too dark in this chamber to really find your way around. Drat! You'll have to paddle back out and try to find another wa—

There's something in the water.

An enormous hump and fins are silhouetted by the light from the tunnel entrance. They're waaaay too big to belong to a salmon. Are they keeping whales—or sharks—in here?

No. Ridiculous. You're in a river.

Either way, time to get out of here. You start paddling faster, eyes on the mouth of the cave. You hear something break the surface of the water behind you, but you don't look back.

Clunk. Your paddle hits something, and it isn't the riverbed.

Don't look back!

Just keep your eyes on the prize, you tell yourself. *Get out, get to shore, find another way in . . .*

There! You've made it back to the river.

SPLASH!

A monstrous fish breaches the water. It's easily the size of a great white shark, but it's blue and red, with eyes the size of basketballs. It's an impossibly giant salmon!

The fish monster splashes back into the water, and now it's swimming right towards the canoe.

With growing horror, you watch it speed towards you underwater. You can't outrun this thing. Not in a canoe.

SPLASH!

The salmon breaches again, jaw agape. You stare into its giant open mouth. If you don't act fast, you're going to be this thing's next meal.

You've got no weapon, except . . .

Your paddle.

Or the flare gun you brought along.

No time to think. Act now.

Where's your luck?
The flare gun? Turn to page 117.
Or the paddle? Turn to page 115.

04:38

There's no telling what's beyond that rusty grate, even if it is just a bunch of fish. You decide to find another way up to the top of the dam.

You bank the canoe and pull it ashore, then turn your head skyward. All you see in your field of vision is the dam and the sky. How are you possibly going to get up there?

You move away from the dam wall and follow a muddy path edging the mountainside. It winds along the river for a little bit, then the river continues downstream while the path reaches around a rocky outcrop.

Cautiously, you peer around the outcrop. The path continues to line the rocky edge, but it's less muddy there. You follow it, and voila! You're standing outside a doorway built into the mountainside.

"That was easy," you say to yourself. Good thing you didn't go in that creepy underground chamber.

You reach out to open the door, and—

BLANG! BLANG! BLANG!

You've tripped an alarm system.

That was also easy.

You whirl around to make your escape, but you hear a motor on the river. A second later a Zodiac zooms downstream with at least five armed guards on board.

You stop and raise your hands high above your head.

You were looking for a way out of these woods, and you certainly found it. In a few short moments, you're put into handcuffs, taken through the door, marched down several sets of stairs, and thrown into a dingy cell.

"Don't I get a phone call?" you blurt out to the guards, who haven't spoken to you once.

You're answered with a door shutting you in.

Slowly, you sink to the floor of the cell.

You get the feeling that this secret base will stay a secret, and that you're about to become a permanent resident...

THE END.

To try again, go back to page 4.

01:43

John's way too tough for you to take one-on-one. You reach into your pocket and feel for the pocket knife. You can fling it at John to startle him, and maybe even knock the remote control from his hands.

Maybe, but it's a fifty-fifty shot.

Go to page 19 . . .

. . . or to page 21.

`02:46`

You can barely keep the paddle upright in your sweaty, shaking hands. You watch with a mixture of fascination and blood-draining horror as the massive maw of the salmon grows larger and larger in your field of vision.

Time slows to a standstill. You gulp, waiting until you can't see anything but the salmon's ribbed gullet. This may be the last thing you ever see . . .

You reach out—

CRUNCH!

You close your eyes. Instinctively, you shield your body. And breathe.

"What the—?"

You open your eyes. The salmon is bobbing above the surface, the paddle wedged between its giant jaws.

"IT WORKED?"

The salmon splashes in the water. It thrashes its head from side to side, trying to shake the paddle out of its mouth, but you wedged it in there really well.

Now's your chance. You leap from the canoe and begin swimming like mad to the water's edge.

You listen to the thrashing behind you. *Please let that paddle hold. Just a few more seconds . . .*

SNAP!

Oh no! You turn in time to see the salmon's jaws shut. The leviathan descends under the water, except for a lone dorsal fin that follows you.

You turn back. Time to give that Olympic-level swim of your life! You paddle. You kick. You're pretty sure your feet are hitting the head of the fish. You don't even breathe. Your muscles just push and push, and then you're grabbing dry land. You heave yourself up onto the shore.

You roll over and watch with horror as the fish springs at you, mouth agape, and—

MISSES.

You keep rolling along, watching as the semi-beached fish pushes itself back into the water, a dark shape in a dark river. You've done it!

Shakily, you pull yourself back onto two legs and let out a deep breath. You survived, but now you've got to press on. Your mind spins with thoughts of what Prisha might be up to at this place. It can't be good, and you don't need to think about saving her anymore. You've got to find your way back to your group, only now you're cold, wet and in the middle of the mountainous woods.

The next adventure is just beginning . . .

00:00

You survived! There are ten other ways to escape the danger— try to find them all!

02:46

This flare gun's got to be good for something. Like blowing up a giant salmon. The only problem is you've never fired one before. How hard could it be?

You wobble unsteadily in the boat, aiming at the approaching leviathan. You put all of your weight forward, pull the trigger, and—

F-SHOOM! The flare shoots out of the gun, arcs wildly, and fizzles out as it hits the water.

"NO!" you scream, as you're thrown out of the canoe.

Of course, the salmon follows through. It comes down on the canoe, cracking it in half.

No time to look back. You'll have to swim. You reach out with your arms, kick wildly with your legs. You manage a stroke. Another stroke. You begin to propel your body through the water. Wow! You're doing it! You're actually going to outrun a mutant salmon!

A dark shape comes rushing up from the depths. The salmon's massive jaws spring open. Its huge eyes lock on to your flailing, thrashing body.

GULP!

THE END.
To try again, go back to page 4.

03:33

"**G**RRNGNRGR!" it shouts again. It's waving and pointing downstream.

You turn and see a cloud of mist. Mist? It's a clear day. The only way you'd get mist in this kind of weather would be from a—

"Waterfall!" you blurt.

"GRGRNNNGRRR!" the sasquatch blurts back.

"Right!" you say. "GRGRNNNGRRR!"

It jumps up and down excitedly.

"No way!" you say to yourself, as the sasquatch grabs your paddle and pulls you to shore.

You jump out of the canoe as the speedy current takes the boat. You stare dumbfounded at your rescuer, then turn to see the canoe go over what has to be a massive waterfall.

Now it's just you, a sasquatch and no canoe.

You gulp. Your heart begins to race as you stare up at its three-metre frame.

The sasquatch looks at you and narrows its eyes. "Grrngnrrrg," it says.

"Uh . . ." you say.

It reaches out with its huge, hairy hand . . .

You scream.

Then you realize: it's patting you on the shoulder.

"Grrnrgnrg," it says.

"Uh . . ." you say again.

It points to you. "Uhhhh," it says. Then it points to itself. "Grrngrr."

"Grrngrr?"

The sasquatch gives an excited grunt. Is it telling you its name?

"Grrngrr?" you ask.

"Uhhhh," it says, and points to you. Then the sasquatch takes you by the hand and leads you into the forest. You think about turning and running, but what good will that do? The sasquatch is bigger and stronger, and it knows these woods inside and out.

Besides, if it really wanted to kill you, wouldn't it have done so already?

You walk several paces behind it. The sasquatch continues to look over its shoulder, nodding at you and beckoning for you to follow. "Uhhhh," it repeats.

"Sure thing," you say.

Then, just as the woods are getting really thick and buggy, the sasquatch stops. It turns to you and puts a finger to your lips.

A moment later you hear the crackling of twigs. Several tall, dark shapes appear from all sides. You gulp. You're about to open your mouth to scream, but you think better of it.

It's a whole family of sasquatches. One of them is even cradling a little baby sasquatch.

Grrngrr turns to the others, points at you, and gives what you can only imagine is a big sasquatch grin. "Uhhhh."

"UHHHH," all of the sasquatches say in unison.

"Oh, great," you sigh. "Guys, my name is really . . ."

00:00

You survived! (Sort of. Now you're stuck with a sasquatch family.) There are ten other ways to escape the danger—try to find them all!

03:33

"**N**o way!" you yell, as if the sasquatch understands English. Now the hairy giant is jumping around excitedly and pointing into the distance.

"GRRNG! GRRNG! GRNNGNR!" it grrrngnrs.

"GRRNG YOURSELF!" you snap. The sasquatch stops making noises and just stares downstream.

That's when you notice how loud that rushing water has become. It's deafening.

You turn and stare at the river, only—

Only there isn't any more river. It's just a cloud of mist.

"Oh no," you say to yourself, but it's too late to paddle out of the way.

And then the canoe pitches forward, and you're staring down a waterfall that's as high as a skyscraper.

Your stomach feels like it's rocketing into your throat. You open your mouth to scream as gravity takes over, pushing the canoe down, then—

Water—

Rushing—

Rocks—

THE END.

To try again, go back to page 4.

07:37

You look down—way down—at the drop beside you. What kind of incline is that? Sixty degrees?

As a kid you always rolled down hills, but not this steep and not full of massive tree trunks that your head could slam into.

ZAP!

John's way too trigger happy with that laser gun.

You stop running and, without missing a beat, yell out, "Cannonball!"

And then you drop.

WHUMP—WHUMP—WHUMP—WHUMP— WHUMP—

The mountainside is a whirl of motion as you spin. You open your mouth to scream, but it fills with a sickening mixture of old pine needles and wet moss—and possibly some moose droppings thrown in for good measure.

You hear more zaps, but they're fainter now.

Then—*OOOF!* You collide with a hefty tree trunk.

You stop suddenly and your limbs flail helplessly. You have no sense of up or down as the world around you continues to spin like a top.

You hear John starting to make his way down the mountain towards you.

Focus, you tell yourself. It hurts to breathe. You've probably cracked a rib or three, but you'll worry about that later. If there *is* a later.

You look down the mountainside. Yikes, you're barely halfway there.

And down you go again.

This time you manage to dodge the trees, or maybe you're just moving so quickly that you obliterate anything in your path. Who knows?

And then the ground shifts from dirt to something harder. Much harder.

You come to a stop. You're lying face down with your mouth pressed against the hard surface of . . .

"A road!" you croak.

Yes, a road. Shakily you get to your feet. The world is still spinning too quickly for you to take it all in.

But amid the wobbly sensation, you notice a rumbling.

A deep, heavy rumbling.

Then the blaring of a horn.

Headlights.

Maybe more of them than you should be seeing. They're bearing down on you.

You hear the squeal of brakes. Tires skidding.

A truck.

You hold out your hands. Go away, truck!

You open your mouth to scream, but the truck squeals to a halt.

The door is flung open. *RCMP* is emblazoned on its side.

"Police!" you say in amazement.

And sure enough, out steps an officer. She's wearing a cap and uniform, though not in the traditional blazing red of the Royal Canadian Mounted Police. But she's a cop and she's armed—exactly what you need right now.

You try to explain more, but you're completely out of breath and panting like you've just tumbled down a mountainside or something.

"Easy, easy," the officer says. She looks at the terrain surrounding you. "You must be that kid who got lost on the canoe trip, right?"

You nod.

"We picked up a distress call from the rest of your camp," she says. "How did you get out this far?"

"It's a long story," you say.

But you're safe for now, and you'll be able to rescue Prisha.

00:00

You survived! There are ten other ways to escape the danger— try to find them all!

07:37

Those rocks are just within reach. As long as you keep zigzagging, John won't be able to keep his laser trained on you.

Then another laser beam whizzes by, this time grazing the side of your foot. You let out a yelp and drop to the ground.

You gasp for breath, only now realizing how spent your body is from running up the steep hill.

"Come on, kid," John yells. "You won't be able to outrun me. That's why I was picked for this mission. I survive. And I eliminate any obstacle in my way."

No, you can't outrun him, but hiding behind the boulders will buy you some time to figure out how to escape.

You bolt as fast as your feet will take you, although you're limping from your wound. It's like someone stabbed you with a red-hot poker . . . or, better still, like someone *blasted you in the foot with a flippin' LASER BEAM!*

You try your best to ignore the pain. If you can just get around to the other side of that boulder, you'll be all right.

ZAP!

You whip around to see John with his laser raised and pointed.

You jump to the side as John fires again. Then you pull yourself up and jump behind the boulder.

Now you're safe, at least for the time being.

If you keep moving along the rock wall, maybe you can get the slip on this guy.

Pressing your back against the boulder, you edge around. You can still hear laser blasts. *Silly fool,* you think. *He's wasting his time shooting at me from the other side of this rock.*

Your thoughts are cut short by a heavy rumbling.

It's coming from overhead.

Oh, you realize. John wasn't aiming at you. He was aiming at the rocks above your head.

Here they come, fast. Downward. And right at you.

THE END.

To try again, go back to page 48.

08:28

You did the rapids before; you can do them again.

To keep from toppling out of the canoe, you duck so that you're almost lying down.

BOOF! BAM! The canoe cracks and scrapes against boulders, shuddering with each heavy blow.

"Please hold together," you hiss between clenched teeth.

Rocks and boulders batter the boat. Heavy waves drench you in an ice-cold bath. Your teeth chatter from the cold and fear. And then . . .

The roar of raging water subsides.

You raise your head to look. The rapids have vanished. In their place is an unbroken stream of water pushing you along a winding path through the forest.

You quickly sit up and pull the paddle out. Shakily, you dip it in and out of the water, trying to get your bearings. After all, there's no way you'll be able to go back the way you came.

The river takes another turn, and then you see it.

A MASSIVE DAM stretches across a wide mountain pass. It's a wall of concrete at least a hundred metres high. It's got to be as big as the Hoover Dam, but you've never heard of this place before. How can that be?

Weird.

You crane your head up and notice something even weirder.

A shadowy figure is sneaking across the top of the dam. You squint and then gasp. It's Prisha! What's she doing up there? She's certainly not moving like she's hurt.

You paddle closer to get a better look.

Now Prisha's lowering something onto a ledge jutting out of the dam's side. What could it be?

Whatever she's doing, she lied about being hurt, and now she's being sneaky on this mystery dam.

You could confront her, but how are you going to get up there?

You paddle over to the edge of the structure. It's not just concrete. There are ledges and grates along the sides. And there are other walls and entrances as well, including a grate against the mountainside with water running through it and a sign above it: *KEEP OUT. SALMON TEST GROUP B.*

Salmon! Why would anyone need to keep away from such yummy fish?

The grate doesn't look locked, and there's just more water inside. Maybe you can paddle in and look for a way to get up to Prisha? Or maybe you should listen to the sign and look elsewhere.

If you open the grate and paddle in, turn to page 110.

If you find another way to the dam, turn to page 112.

06:24

You visualize your legs moving in perfect circles as you sprint, Olympian-like, to the door. Then you kick your legs out in front of you and drop into a slide. Your shoes squeal against the tile floor, and friction burns the underside of your legs.

There are only a few centimetres between safety and having your head caught in the door.

You close your eyes and—

SLAM.

Death comes hard and fast. And then you think to yourself: *I'm thinking! Does that happen after death?*

Then you begin to notice other things, like the fact that you're still breathing from your lungs, which are connected to your head, which has *not* been crushed to a pulp by the door.

"Yes!" you snap. "I rule! Safe at first base!"

"What are you doing here?" a voice hisses.

You look up. Prisha is standing above you, arms folded across her chest. She looks about as happy as someone who's just been doused with a bucket of goat barf.

You're both in the middle of a cavernous room. In fact, it *is* a cavern! The walls are rough rock face, and the domed ceiling extends high above Prisha's head.

And there's definitely water in this cave. Beyond Prisha, you notice a dock where several Jet Skis are moored.

"Are you even listening?" Prisha growls.

"Don't get angry with me," you say, standing up. "You're the one who faked being hurt."

"I *was* hurt," Prisha says. "I just have my ... priorities."

"Like what? Sneaking into this place? And dropping that bomb on the ledge back there?"

Prisha's eyes widen. She checks a diver's watch on her wrist. "You're right," she says hurriedly. "I've got to get moving."

"Where are we going?"

"*We?* Oh no. You were meant to be stuck back at the canoe looking for help, and hopefully lost in the woods far away from here."

"What are you even talking about, Prisha?"

"I'm not Prisha," she tells you. "I work for an organization that's trying to stop this horrible place by whatever means necessary. I'm sorry," she continues, "but you're on your own." Then she pushes past you, running towards the dock.

Prisha leaps aboard one of the Jet Skis, reaches into a pouch at her side for a knife, and cuts the line holding it there. She turns the Jet Ski on and races into a tunnel ahead.

Then the entire cave shakes. You're nearly thrown

off your feet. Above, rocks shake free from the ceiling and hurtle towards you.

The bomb! It must have exploded, and it's shaking this whole place apart.

You start running, dodging rocks and boulders as jagged cracks form along the walls. The water by the dock is heaving with large waves. You don't have much time.

You race over to the dock, which is coming apart in pieces. You're no American Ninja Warrior, but you're going to have to run across the fragmenting dock like it's one of those obstacle courses if you want to get to one of the other Jet Skis.

"Ninja!" you scream, and run over bits and pieces of dock. You get across in three steps, then leap aboard the Jet Ski.

It's a good thing you've got that pocket knife. You cut the rope and fiddle with the controls until the engine roars to life.

Rocks continue to rain down around you, splashing into the water and sending massive waves in every direction. You've got to get out of here, and fast. You bear down on the throttle and zoom into the tunnel after Prisha.

Turn to the next page.

04:00

The Jet Ski jumps the waves caused by the bomb blast. Your butt keeps slamming on and off the seat. If you survive this, you're going to have the world's most serious case of chafing.

Looking ahead, you see Prisha's silhouette against the daylight streaming in the other end of the tunnel. Then she veers sharply to the left.

Thirty seconds later you emerge from the tunnel into the wide lake, just as huge chunks of concrete come crashing down, blocking the tunnel behind you.

You're out!

Where's Prisha?

Suddenly, you see a blur of motion as Prisha's Jet Ski speeds towards you.

She zooms past, but her wake is big enough to send your Jet Ski airborne.

You try to regain control, but the Jet Ski is already twisting in mid-air. Do you try to land this jump?

If you hang on, turn to page 92.
If you let go, turn to page 93.

At full height, the bear is bigger than the sasquatch, and hopefully slower.

You've played countless games of tag; this is basically the same. You just don't want to get tagged It by the grizzly.

You let out a piercing scream to startle it. Bad idea. The bear stops, looks your way, and takes a swipe.

But that's also when you make your move. You dodge the blow and scramble past it.

Nice! You're doing it again—succeeding in the face of certain doom—and once again you wish that someone was recording this for posterity, when—

WHUMP! You slam face first onto the ground.

You flip over. "Tree root!" you yell. That's what tripped you? A stupid, useless tree root!

A shadow falls over your head.

You look up into the giant maw of the angry bear.

On second thought, maybe you shouldn't have screamed at it. You watch as it rears back, then slices forward through the air with those razor-sharp claws.

SWISH!

THE END.

To try again, go back to page 4.

02:32

You're gonna blow this place sky high!

Using both hands, you turn the two keys to switch on the self-destruct mechanism.

Instantly the room is bathed in angry red light.

Sirens begin to blare.

"SELF-DESTRUCT CODE ACTIVATED," a computerized voice booms.

On the monitors, you see Prisha and her captors reeling about.

People begin to scramble.

Wow, blowing this place up was super easy!

You grab the keys from the self-destruct switches and jam them into your pocket. There's no turning back now!

Sneaking one last look at the monitors, you see that the guards have forgotten about Prisha and are trying to get out of this place.

Good idea. You race out of the room only to encounter scores of people moving in every direction. Where did they all come from?

You're not sure where to go, so you pick a lab-coated scientist and follow him. He's scrambling down a corridor that's already jammed with people.

"BASE WILL SELF-DESTRUCT IN T MINUS TWO

MINUTES," the voice says in a tone that is way too calm for anything that's about to self-destruct.

Heart thumping in your chest, you try to squeeze past the lineup, but you're getting nowhere.

Then a hand grabs your wrist tightly and pulls you out of the line.

"Prisha!" you shout.

"Thanks for your help back there," she says.

"How did you know it was me?"

"Who else would set off the self-destruct sequence in this place? But enough of that. I know a quicker way out of here. Come with me."

You look at the lineup, debating for a second. Then you shrug. "Let's go!"

Amazingly, Prisha leads you away from the flow of traffic.

"Don't these guys know the right way to get out of here?" you ask.

"Sure," Prisha says. "The official way. But I'm here unofficially."

She looks down at her watch, then comes to a stop. "Cover your ears," she says.

"Why?"

That's when you hear—and feel—a huge *BOOM!*

Prisha uncovers her ears, then looks you in the eye. "That present I left earlier? It's our escape hatch!"

She grabs you by the wrist again and pulls you over

to one of the doors in the hallway. It's marked with a green light.

Prisha flings the door open, and you run after her into a room that is falling to pieces. The ceiling has cracked. Electrical equipment sparks. Lights and other equipment dangle from frayed wires and cords.

A knee-high torrent of water rushes across the floor and out a MASSIVE HOLE IN THE WALL.

Daylight is streaming in. You're at the spot on the ledge where Prisha had set the charges. Now you understand why.

"But how are we going to get out of here?" you blurt. "It's still, like, a two-hundred-metre drop to the river!"

And then, through the hole in the wall, you hear the sound of a massive engine.

Suddenly a helicopter lowers into view.

You look at Prisha.

She looks at you. "Yes, we've got to jump this one."

You stare at the canyon below. There's no way you can make a jump like that.

And then she's off. You watch as she runs through the water on the floor, then leaps across the chasm and grabs hold of a rope ladder hanging from the chopper's landing skid.

"No way," you say, watching her scramble up. Once she's in the cockpit, she waves you on.

"No way," you say again, but what choice do you have?

You gulp. Then mustering all of your strength, and madness, you make a run for it.

The water is totally slowing you down, but you pump your legs and your fists, and then you see the ground drop away.

You sail through the air, watching as the helicopter comes closer, closer—

You reach out and—

Catch the ladder by the very last rung.

Then you feel a massive blast of hot air.

The base is exploding!

The helicopter swerves to avoid the huge fireball, but you're still dangling from the ladder, tossed about like a rag doll.

You grip the ladder more tightly than you've ever gripped anything before.

A massive tsunami of water pours into the canyon, filling out the thin trickle of a river below.

The helicopter rights itself and flies along the flow of the water. You watch in amazement, not sure if you've chosen the right side—after all, you've just helped Prisha destroy a top-secret base.

All in a day's work, you figure.

00:00

You survived! There are ten other ways to escape the danger—try to find them all!

02:32

You're brave, but you're not crazy. You plop into one of the chairs positioned around the monitors and find a computer that has an internet browser. Then you use it to contact 9-1-1.

The dispatch operator picks up, and you begin to explain your situation to her. "I'm in this base. It's attached to—or maybe even inside—this huge dam."

"Sorry, what is your location?" the operator asks.

"Uhh . . ." You were lost. That's the whole point. "Can't you trace this call?"

Silence. "You're using a computer to contact us?"

"Yes, exactly. I broke into their security room. The people here are dangerous. You've got to send help!"

"We're trying," the operator says, "but we can't get a lock on the location. You're using a computer with an untraceable server."

"A what?" You look around the room. Everything is done through computer here. The place is totally sealed off, communications-wise.

Your own cellphone? There's no way you could get a signal this far down in the base.

"Can you describe anything else about your location?" the operator asks. You begin to explain where your